Frank Herbert

Mr. Herbert is the author of The DUNE Trilogy and many other acclaimed SF works. Born in Tacoma, Washington, Mr. Herbert served in the U.S. Navy in World War II. He has worked as a photographer, television cameraman, radio newsman, oyster diver, and psychoanalyst. He has also taught creative writing. He lives in the state of Washington with his family.

THE
GODMAKERS

FRANK HERBERT

BERKLEY BOOKS, NEW YORK

This Berkley book contains the complete
text of the original hardcover edition.
It has been completely reset in a type face
designed for easy reading, and was printed
from new film.

THE GODMAKERS

A Berkley Book / published by arrangement with
G. P. Putnam's Sons

PRINTING HISTORY
G. P. Putnam's Sons edition published 1972
Berkley edition / September 1978
Thirteenth printing / April 1982

ISBN: 0-425-05516-7

A BERKLEY BOOK ® TM 757,375
Berkley Books are published by Berkley Publishing Corporation,
200 Madison Avenue, New York, New York 10016.
The name "BERKLEY" and the stylized "B" with design
are trademarks belonging to Berkley Publishing Corporation.
PRINTED IN THE UNITED STATES OF AMERICA

You must understand that peace is an internal matter. It has to be a self-discipline for an individual or for an entire civilization. It must come from within. If you set up an outside power to enforce peace, this outside power will grow stronger and stronger. It has no alternative. The inevitable outcome will be an explosion, cataclysmic and chaotic. That is the way of our universe. When you create paired opposites, one will overwhelm the other unless they are in delicate balance.

—*The writings of* **DIANA BULLONE**

To become a god, a living creature must transcend the physical. The three steps of this transcendent path are known. First, he must come upon the awareness of secret aggression. Second, he must come upon .the discernment of purpose within the animal shape. Third, he must experience death.

When this is done, the nascent god must find his own rebirth in a unique ordeal by which he discovers the one who summoned him.

"The Making of a God,"
The Amel Handbook

Lewis Orne could not remember a time when he had been free of a peculiar, repetitive dream, when he had been able to go to sleep in the sure knowledge that the dream's wild sense of reality would not clutch at his psyche.

The dream began with music, this really hokey unseen choir, syrup in sound, a celestial joke. Vaporous figures would come out of the music adding a visual dimension of the same quality. Finally, a voice would override the whole silly thing with disturbing pronouncements:

"Gods are made, not born!"

Or:

"To say you are neutral is another way of saying

7

you accept the necessities of war!"

To look at him, you wouldn't think him the kind of person to be plagued by such a dream. He was a blocky human with the thick muscles of a heavy planet native—Chargon of Gemma was his birthplace. He possessed a face reminiscent of a full-jowled bulldog and a steady gaze which often made people uncomfortable.

Despite his peculiar dream, or perhaps because of it, Orne made regular obeisance to Amel, "the planet where all godness dwells." Because of the dream's pronouncements, which remained with him all through his waking life, he enlisted on the morning of his nineteenth birthday in the Rediscovery and Reeducation Service, thereby seeking to reknit the galactic empire shattered by the Rim Wars.

After training him in the great Peace School on Marak, R&R set Orne down one cloudy morning on the meridian longitude, fortieth parallel, of the newly rediscovered planet of Hamal, terra type to eight decimal places, the occupants sufficiently close to the homo-S genetic drift for interbreeding with natives of the Heart Worlds.

Ten Hamal weeks later, as he stood at the edge of a dusty little village in the planet's North Central Uplands, Orne pushed the panic button of the little green signal unit in his right-hand jacket pocket. At the moment, he was intensely aware that he was the lone representative on Hamal of a service which often lost agents to "causes unknown."

What had sent his hand thrusting for the signal unit was the sight of about thirty Hamalites continuing to stare with brooding gloom at a companion who had just executed a harmless accidental pratfall into a mound of soft fruit.

No laughter, no discernible change of emotion.

Added to all the other items Orne had cataloged, the incident of the pratfall-in-the-fruit compounded Hamal's aura of doom.

Orne sighed. It was done. He had sent a signal out into space, set a chain of events into motion which could result in the destruction of Hamal, of himself, or both.

As he was to discover later, he had also rid himself of his repetitive dream, replacing it with a sequence of waking events which would in time make him suspect he had walked into his mysterious night world.

A religion requires numerous dichotomic relationships. It needs believers and unbelievers. It needs those who know the mysteries and those who only fear them. It needs the insider and the outsider. It needs both a god and a devil. It needs absolutes and relativity. It needs that which is formless (though in the process of forming) and that which is formed.

—*Religious Engineering,*
secret writings of Amel

"We are about to make a god," Abbod Halmyrach said.

He was a short, dark-skinned man in a pale-orange robe that fell to his ankles in soft folds. His face, narrow and smooth, was dominated by a long nose that hung like a precipice over a wide, thin-lipped mouth. His head was polished brown baldness.

"We do not know from what creature or *thing* the god will be born," the Abbod said. "It could be one of you."

He gestured to the room full of acolytes seated on the bare floor of an austere room illuminated by the flat rays of Amel's midmorning sun. The room was a Psi fortress buttressed by instruments and spells. It measured twenty meters to the side, three meters floor to ceiling. Eleven windows, five on one side and six on the other, looked out across the park rooftops of Amel's central warren complex. The wall behind the Abbod and the one he faced gave the appearance of white stone laced with thin brown lines like insect tracks—one of the configurations of a Psi machine. The walls glowed with pale-white light as flat as skimmed milk.

The Abbod felt the force flowing between these two walls and experienced the anticipatory flash of guilt-fear which he knew was shared by the acolyte class. Officially, this class was called Religious Engineering, but the young acolytes persisted in their impiety. To them, this was God Making.

And they were sufficiently advanced to know the perils.

"What I say and do here has been planned and measured out with precision," the Abbod said. "Random influence is dangerous here. That is why this room is so purposefully plain. The smallest extraordinary intrusion here could bring immeasurable differences into what we do. I say, then, that no shame attaches to any one of you who wishes at this time to leave this room and not participate in the making of a god."

The seated acolytes stirred beneath their white robes, but no one accepted his invitation.

The Abbod experienced a small sensation of satisfaction. Thus far, things went within the range of his predictions. He said:

"As we know, the danger in making a god is that we succeed. In the science of Psi, a success on the order of magnitude which we project in this room carries profound reflexive peril. We do, in fact, make a god. Having made a god, we achieve something paradoxically no longer our creation. We could well become the creation of that which we create."

The Abbod nodded to himself, reflecting on the god creations in humankind's history: wild, purposeful, primitive, sophisticated . . . but all unpredictable. No matter how made, the god went his own way. God whims were not to be taken lightly.

"The god comes anew each time out of chaos," the Abbod said. "We do not control this; we only know how to make a god."

He felt the dry electricity of fear building in his mouth, recognized the necessary tension growing around him. The god must come partly out of fear, but not alone from fear.

"We must stand in awe of our creation," he said. "We must be ready to adore, to obey, to plead and supplicate."

The acolytes knew their cue. "Adore and obey,"

they murmured. Awe radiated from them.

Ah, yes, the Abbod thought; *infinite possibilities and infinite peril, that is where we now stand. The fabric of our universe is woven into these moments.*

He said: "First, we call into being the demishape, the agent of the god we would create." He lifted his arms, breaking the force flow between the two walls, setting eddies adrift in the room. As he moved, he felt a simultaneity, a time-rift in his universe with the image-awareness within him that told of three things happening together. A vision of his own brother, Ag Emolirdo, came into his mind, a long-nosed, birdlike human standing in pale light on faraway Marak, sobbing without cause. This vision flowed into the image of a hand, one finger depressing a button on a small green box. In the same instant, he saw himself standing with arms upraised as a Shriggar, the Chargonian death lizard, stepped from the Psi wall behind him.

The acolytes gasped.

With the exquisite slowness of terror, the Abbod lowered his arms, turned. Yes, it was a true Shriggar—a creature so tall it must crouch in this room. Great scratching talons drooped from its short arms. The narrow head with its hooked beak open to reveal a forked tongue twisted left, then right. Its stalk eyes wriggled and its breath filled the room with swamp odors.

Abruptly, the mouth snapped closed: "*Chunk!*"

When it reopened, a voice issued from it: deep, disembodied, articulated without synchronization of Shriggar tongue and lips. It said:

"The god you make may die aborning. Such things take their own time and their own way. I stand watchful and ready. There will be a game of war, a city of

12

glass where creatures of high potential make their lives. There will be a time for politics and a time for priests to fear the consequences of their daring. All of this must be to achieve an unknown goal."

Slowly, the shriggar began to dissolve—first the head, then the great yellow-scaled body. A puddle of warm brown fluid formed where it had stood, oozed across the room, around the Abbod's feet, around the seated acolytes.

None of them dared move. They knew better than to introduce a random force of their own into this place before the flickering Psi currents subsided.

Anyone who has ever felt his skin crawl with the electrifying awareness of an unseen presence knows the primary sensation of Psi.

—HALMYRACH, ABBOD OF AMEL,
Psi and Religion, Preface

Lewis Orne clasped his hands behind his back until the knuckles showed white. He stared darkly out of his second-story window at a Hamal morning. The big yellow sun dominated a cloudless sky above distant mountains. It promised to be a scorcher of a day.

Behind him there was the sound of a scratchy stylus rasping across transmit-paper as the Investigation-Adjustment operative made notes on the interview they had just completed. The paper was transmitting a record of the words to the operative's waiting ship.

So maybe I was wrong to push the panic button, Orne thought. *That doesn't give this wise guy the right to ride me! After all, this is my first job. They can't expect perfection the first time out.*

The scratching stylus began to wear on Orne's nerves.

Creases furrowed Orne's square forehead. He put his left hand up to the rough wooden window frame, ran his right hand through the stiff bristles of his close-cropped red hair. The loose cut of his white coverall uniform—standard for R&R agents—accentuated his blocky appearance. Blood suffused his full-jowled face. He felt himself vacillating between anger and the urge to give full vent to a pixie nature which he usually kept under control.

He thought: *If I'm wrong about this place, they'll boot me out of the service. There's too much bad blood between R&R and Investigation-Adjustment. This I-A joker would just love to make us look stupid. But by god! There'll be some jumping if I'm right about Hamal!*

Orne shook his head. *But I'm probably wrong.*

The more he thought about it, the more he felt it had been stupid to call in the I-A. Hamal probably was not aggressive by nature. Very likely there was no danger that R&R would provide the technological basis for arming a potential war maker.

Still . . .

Orne sighed. He felt a vague, dreamlike uneasiness. The sensation reminded him of the drifting awareness before awakening, the moments of clarity when action, thought and emotion combined.

14

Someone clumped down the stairs at the other end of the building. The floor shook beneath Orne's feet. This was an old building, the government guesthouse, built of rough lumber. The room carried the sour smell of many former occupants and haphazard cleaning.

From his second floor window Orne could see part of the cobblestone market square of this village of Pitsiben. Beyond the square he could make out the wide track of the ridge road that came up from the Plains of Rogga. Along the road stretched a double line of moving figures: farmers and hunters coming for market day in Pitsiben. Amber dust hung over the road. It softened the scene, imparted a romantic out-of-focus look.

Farmers leaned into the pushing harnesses of their low two-wheeled carts, plodding along with a heavy-footed swaying motion. They wore long green coats, yellow berets tipped uniformly over the left ear, yellow trousers with cuffs darkened by the road dust, open sandals that revealed horny feet splayed out like the feet of draft animals. Their carts were piled high with green and yellow vegetables seemingly arranged to carry out the general pastel color scheme.

Brown-clothed hunters moved with the line, but at one side like flank guards. They strode along, heads high, cap feathers bobbing. Each carried a bell-muzzled fowling piece at a jaunty angle over one arm, a spyglass in a leather case over the left shoulder. Behind the hunters trotted their apprentices pulling three-wheeled game carts overflowing with tiny swamp deer, dappleducks and *porjos*, the snake-tailed rodents which Hamalites considered such a delicacy.

On the distant valley floor Orne could see the dark-red spire of the I-A ship that had come flaming down just after dawn on this day, homing on his transmitter. The ship, too, seemed set in a dream haze, its shape clouded by blue smoke from kitchen fires in the farm homes that dotted the valley. The ship's red shape towered above the homes, looking out of place, an ornament left over from holiday decorations for giants.

As Orne watched, a hunter paused on the ridge road, unlimbered his spyglass, studied the I-A ship. The hunter appeared only vaguely curious. His action didn't fit expectations; it just didn't fit.

The smoke and hot yellow sun conspired to produce a summery appearance to the countryside—a look of lush growing behind pastel heat. It was essentially a peaceful scene, arousing in Orne a deep feeling of bitterness.

Damn! I don't care what the I-A says. I was right to call them. These Hamalites are hiding something. They're not peaceful. The real mistake here was made by that dumbo on First-Contact when he gabbled about the importance we place on a peaceful history!

Orne grew aware that the scratching of the stylus had stopped. The I-A man cleared his throat.

Orne turned, looked across the low room at the operative. The I-A agent sat at a rough table beside Orne's unmade bed. Papers and folders were scattered all around him on the table. A small recorder weighted one stack. The I-A man slouched in a bulky wooden chair. He was big-headed, gangling and with overlarge features, a leathery skin. His hair was dark and straggling. The eyelids drooped. They gave to his face that look of haughty superciliousness that was like a brand mark of the I-A. The man wore patched blue fatigues without insignia. He had introduced himself as Umbo

16

Stetson, chief I-A operative for this sector.

The chief operative, Orne thought. *Why'd they send the chief operative?*

Stetson noted Orne's attention, said: "I believe we have most of it now. Let's just check it over once more for luck. You landed here ten weeks ago, right?"

"Yes. I was set down by a landing boat from the R&R transport, Arneb Rediscovery."

"This was your first mission?"

"I told you that. I graduated from Uni-Galacta with the class of '07, and did my apprentice work on Timurlain."

Stetson frowned. "Then they sent you right out here to this newly rediscovered backwash planet?"

"That's right."

"I see. And you were full of the old rah-rah, the old missionary spirit to uplift mankind, all that sort of thing."

Orne blushed, scowled.

Stetson nodded. "I see they're still teaching that 'cultural renaissance' bushwa at dear old Uni-Galacta." He put a hand to his breast, raised his voice in elaborate caricature: "We must reunite the lost planets with the centers of culture and industry, and take up the *glor*-ious onward march of mankind that was cut off so brutally by the Rim Wars!"

He spat on the floor.

"I think we can skip all that," Orne muttered.

"You're sooooo right," Stetson said. "Now, what'd you bring with you to this lovely vacation spot?"

"I had a dictionary compiled by First-Contact, but it was pretty sketchy in . . ."

"Who was that First-Contact?"

"Name on the dictionary says Andre Bullone."

"Oh— Any relation to High Commissioner Bullone?"

"I don't know."

Stetson scribbled something on his papers. "And that First-Contact report says this is a special place, a peaceful planet with a primitive farming-hunting economy, eh?"

"That's right."

"Uh-huh. What else'd you bring into this garden spot?"

"The usual stuff for my job and reports . . . and a transmitter, of course."

"And you pushed the panic button on that transmitter two days ago, eh? Did we get here fast enough for you?"

Orne glared at the floor.

Stetson said: "I suppose you've the usual eidetic memory crammed with cultural-medical-industrial-technological information."

"I'm a fully qualified R&R agent!"

"We will observe a minute of reverent silence," Stetson said. Abruptly, he slammed a hand onto the table. "It's a plain damn stupidity! Nothing but a political come-on!"

Orne snapped to angry attention. "What?"

"This R&R dodge, sonny. It's demagoguery, it's perpetuating a few political lives by endangering all of us. You mark my words: We're going to *re*discover one planet too many; we're going to give its people the industrial foundation they don't deserve; and we're going to see another Rim War to end all Rim Wars!"

Orne took a step forward, glaring. "Why'n hell do you think I pushed the panic button?"

Stetson sat back, his calm restored by the outburst. "My dear fellow, that's what we're now trying to determine." He tapped his front teeth with the stylus. "Now, just why did you call us?"

"I *told* you! It's . . ." He waved a hand at the window.

"You felt lonely and wanted the I-A to come hold your hand, that it?"

"Oh, go to hell!" Orne barked.

"In due time, son. In due time." Stetson's drooping eyelids drooped even farther. "Now . . . just what're they teaching you R&R dummies to look for these days?"

Orne swallowed another angry reply. "War signs."

"What else? But let's be specific."

"We look for fortifications, for war games among the children, for people drilling or other signs of armylike group activities. . . ."

"Such as uniforms?"

"Certainly! And for war scars, wounds on people and buildings, the level of wound treatment knowledge in the medical profession, indications of wholesale destruction—you know, things like that."

"The gross evidence." Stetson shook his head from side to side. "Do you consider this adequate?"

"No, damn it, I don't!"

"You're sooooo right," Stetson said. "Hmmmmmmm. Let's us dig a little deeper. I don't quite understand what bothers you about the honest citizenry here."

Orne sighed, shrugged. "They have no spirit, no bounce. No humor. They live in perpetual seriousness bordering on gloom."

"Oh?"

"Yeah. I . . . I . . . uh . . ." Orne wet his lips with his

tongue. "I . . . uh . . . told the Leaders' Council our people are very interested in a steady source of *froolap* bones for making left-handed bone china saucers."

Stetson jerked forward. "You what?"

"Well, they were so damn serious all the time. I had as much of it as I could take and, well, I . . . uh . . ."

"What happened?"

"They asked for a detailed description of the *froolap* and the accepted method of preparing the bones for shipment."

"What'd you tell them?"

"Well, I . . . Well, according to my description they decided Hamal doesn't have any *froolaps*."

"I see," Stetson said. "That's what's wrong with this place, no *froolaps*."

Now I've done it, Orne thought. *Why can't I keep my big mouth shut? I've just convinced him I'm nuts!*

"Any big cemeteries, national monuments, that sort of thing?" Stetson asked.

"Not a one. But they have this custom where they plant their dead vertically and put an orchard tree over them. There are some mighty big orchards."

"You think that's significant?"

Stetson took a deep breath, leaned back. He tapped his stylus on the table, stared into the distance. Presently, he asked: "How're they taking to reeducation?"

"They're very interested in the industrial end. That's why I'm here in Pitsiben village. We've located a tungsten source nearby and—"

"What about their medical people?" Stetson interrupted. "Wound knowledge, that sort of thing?"

"It's difficult to say," Orne said. "You know how it

is with medics. They have this idea they already know everything and it's difficult to find out just what they *do* know. I'm making progress, though."

"What's their general medical level?"

"They've a good basic knowledge of anatomy, surgery and bone setting. I get no pattern, though, in their knowledge of wounds."

"Do you have any ideas why this planet is so backward?" Stetson asked.

"Their history says Hamal was accidentally seeded by sixteen survivors—eleven women and five men—from a Tritsahin cruiser disabled in an engagement during the early part of the Rim Wars. They landed with a lifeboat without much equipment and damn little know-how. I take it they were mostly black gang who got away."

"And here they sat until R&R came along," Stetson said. "Lovely. Just lovely."

"That was five hundred Standard Years ago," Orne said.

"And these gentle people are still farming and hunting," Stetson murmured. "Oh, lovely." He glared up at Orne. "How long would it take this planet, granting they have the aggressive drive, to become a definite war menace?"

Orne said: "Well—there are two uninhabited planets in the system they could build up for raw materials. Oh, I'd say twenty to twenty-five S'years after they got the industrial foundation on their home planet."

"And how long before the aggressive core would have the know-how to go underground so we'd have to blast the planet apart to get at them?"

"Give 'em a year the way they're going now."

"You are beginning to see the sweet little problem you R&R dummies create for us!" Stetson pointed an accusing finger at Orne. "And let us make one little slip! Let us declare a planet aggressive and bring in an occupation force and let your damn spies find out we made a mistake!" He doubled his hand into a fist. "A-ha!"

"They've already started building factories to produce machine tools," Orne said. "They're quick enough." He shrugged. "They soak everything up like some dark gloomy sponge."

"Very poetic," Stetson growled. He lifted his long frame from the chair, strode to the middle of the room. "Let's go take a closer look. And I'm warning you, Orne, the I-A has more important things to do than go around wet-nursing R&R."

"And you'd just love to make us look like a pack of fumbleheads," Orne said.

"You're sooooo right, son. That would not make me lose any sleep at all."

"So what if I made a mistake! A first . . ."

"We'll see, we'll see. Come along. We'll use my go-buggy."

Here goes nothing, Orne thought. *This schlammer isn't going to look very hard when it's easier to sit back and laugh at R&R. I'm finished before we start.*

One of the essential problems in engineering a religion for any species is to recognize and refrain from inhibiting those self-regulating systems in the species upon which the species' survival depends.

—*Religious Engineering,*
field handbook

It already was beginning to grow hot in Pitsiben when Orne and Stetson emerged onto the cobblestone street. The green and yellow flag drooped limply from its mast atop the guesthouse. All activity seemed to have taken on a slower pace. Groups of stolid Hamalites stood before awning-shaded vegetable stalls across from the guesthouse. They gazed moodily at the I-A vehicle parked at the guesthouse doorway.

The go-buggy was a white basic two-seater teardrop with wraparound window, a turbine in the rear.

Orne and Stetson got in, fastened their safety belts.

"There's what I mean," Orne said.

Stetson started the turbine whining up to power level, engaged the clutch. The buggy bounced several times on the cobbles until the gyro-spring system took hold. It made a neat, flat turn past the vegetable stalls.

Stetson spoke over the turbine sound: "There's what you mean what?"

"Those dolts back there. Any other place in the universe they'd have been around your go-buggy ten deep, prying under the rear vents at the turbine, poking underneath at the suspension. These jerks just stand around at a distance and look gloomy."

"No *froolap*," Stetson said.

"Yeah!"

23

"Why do you think they do that?"

"I think they're obeying orders."

"Why couldn't they just be shy?"

"Forget I mentioned it."

"I see by your reports that there are no walled villages on Hamal," Stetson said. He slowed the buggy to maneuver between two of the low pushcarts. The farmers gave the buggy only a passing glance.

"None that I've seen," Orne said.

"No military drill by large groups?"

"None that I've seen."

"And no heavy armaments?"

"None that I've seen."

"What's this *none-that-I've-seen* kick?" Stetson demanded. "Do you suspect them of hiding something?"

"I do."

"Why?"

"Because things don't seem to fit on this planet. And when things don't fit there are missing pieces."

Stetson took his attention from the street, shot a sharp glance at Orne. "So you're suspicious."

Orne grabbed the door handle as the go-buggy swerved around a corner, headed out onto the wide ridge road. "That's what I told you right at the beginning."

"We're always simply delighted to investigate R&R's slightest suspicions," Stetson said.

"It's better for me to make a mistake than it is for you to make one," Orne growled.

"You will have noticed that their construction is almost entirely of wood," Stetson said. "At their technological level, wood construction leans to the side of peace."

24

"Provided we know what all this means . . ." Orne gestured at the countryside. ". . . in technological level."

"Is that what they're teaching you now at dear old Uni-Galacta?"

"No. That was my own idea. If they have artillery and mobile cavalry, stone forts would be useless."

"What would they use for cavalry?" Stetson asked. "According to your reports, there are no riding animals on Hamal."

"So I haven't found any . . . yet!"

"All right," Stetson said. "I'll be reasonable. You spoke of weapons. What weapons? I haven't seen anything heavier than those fowling pieces carried by their hunters."

"If they had cannon that'd explain a lot of things," Orne said.

"Such as the lack of stone forts?"

"You're damn right!"

"An interesting theory. How do they manufacture the fowling pieces, by the way?"

"They're produced singly by skilled artisans. It's a sort of a guild."

"A sort of a guild. My!" Stetson pulled the go-buggy to a jolting stop on a deserted stretch of the ridge road, shut down the turbine.

Orne stared around him in the silence. It was hot and peaceful. A few hopping insects braved the ridge road's dusty tracks. Orne experienced the disturbing sensation that he had been in just this situation under these precise circumstances before, that he was repeating his life, caught on a circular track from which there was no escape.

"Did First-Contact see any sign of cannon?" Stetson asked.

"You know he didn't."

Stetson nodded. "Mmmmmm, hmmmmm."

"But that could've been accident or design," Orne said. "The stupid *schlammler* shot off his face the first day and told these people how important it is to us that a *redisc* planet have a peaceful society."

"You're sure of that?"

"I've heard the recording."

"Then you're sooooo right," Stetson said. "For once." He slid out of the buggy. "Come on. Give me a hand."

Orne got out of his side. "Why're we stopping?"

Stetson passed him the end of a tape measure. "Hold the idiot end of this at the edge of the road over there like a good fellow, will you?"

Orne obeyed. The plasteel clip at the end of the tape felt cool and dust puffed up between his fingers. The place smelled of earth and musty growing things.

The ridge road proved to be just under seven meters wide. Stetson announced this fact, writing the figure in a notebook. He muttered something about "lines of regression."

They returned to the go-buggy, set off once more down the road.

"What's important about the width of the road?" Orne asked.

"I-A has a profitable sideline selling omnibuses," Stetson said. "I just wanted to see if our current models would fit these roads."

"Funny man!" Orne growled. "I presume it's increasingly difficult for I-A to justify its appropriations."

Stetson laughed. "You're sooooo right! We're going to put in an additional line of nerve tonic for R&R agents. That should get us out of the red."

Orne leaned back into his corner, sank into gloom. *I'm done for. This smart ass chief operative isn't going to find anything I didn't find. There was no real reason for me to call in the I-A except that things don't fit here.*

Stetson turned the go-buggy as the ridge road dipped down to the right through scrub trees.

"We finally get off the high road,"Stetson said.

"If we'd kept straight on we'd have gone down into a swamp," Orne said.

"Oh?"

The road took them out onto the floor of a wide valley cut by lines of windbreak trees. Smoke spiraled into the still air from behind the trees.

"What's that smoke over there?" Stetson asked.

"Farmhouses."

"You've looked?"

"Yes! I've looked!"

"Touchy, aren't we?"

The road took them directly toward a river, crossed it on a crude wooden bridge with stone abutments.

Stetson pulled to a stop on the far side of the bridge, stared at the twin lines of a narrow cart track that wound along the riverbank.

Again they got under way, heading toward another ridge. There were stiled fences beyond the ditches which flanked their road.

"Why do they have fences?" Stetson asked.

27

"To mark their boundaries."

"Why stiles?"

"To keep out the swamp deer," Orne said. "It's reasonable."

"Stiled fences for boundaries and swamp deer," Stetson said. "How big are the swamp deer?"

"Lots of evidence—books, stuffed specimens and the like—to show the biggest of them get about half a meter high."

"And wild."

"Very wild."

"Not a very good suspect as a cavalry animal, Stetson said.

"Definitely ruled out."

"That means you looked into it."

"Thoroughly."

The I-A man pursed his lips in thought, then: "Let's us go over that about their government again."

Orne raised his voice above the whine of the turbine as the buggy began to labor in the climb up to another ridge. "What do you mean?"

"That hereditary business."

"Council membership seems to be passed along on an eldest son basis."

"Seems to be?" Stetson maneuvered the buggy over a steep rise and onto a road that turned right down the crest of the ridge.

Orne shrugged. "Well, they gave me some hanky patanky about an elective procedure in case the eldest son dies and there's no other male heir."

"But definitely patriarchal?"

"Definitely."

"What games do these people play?"

"The children have tops, slingshots, toy carts—but no war toys that I can recognize."

"And the adults?"

"Their games?"

"Yes."

"I've seen one that's played by sixteen men in teams of four. They use a square field about fifty meters to the side. It has smooth diagonal ditches crossing from corner to corner to corner. Four men take stations at each corner and rotate turns at play with . . ."

"Let me guess," Stetson said. "They crawl ferociously at each other along those ditches."

"Very funny! What they do is they use two heavy balls pierced for holding with the fingers. One ball's green and the other's yellow. Yellow ball goes first; it's rolled along the diagonal ditch. The green ball's supposed to be thrown in such a way that it smacks the yellow ball at the intersection."

"And it never hits the yellow ball."

"Sometimes it does. Speed's erratic."

"And a great huzzah goes up when they hit," Stetson said.

"No audience," Orne said.

"None at all?"

"None that . . ."

"I've seen," Stetson chimed in. "Anyway, it appears to be a peaceful game. Are they good at it?"

"Remarkably clumsy, I thought. But they seem to enjoy it. Come to think of it, that game's one of the few things I've ever seen them come close to enjoying."

"You're a frustrated missionary," Stetson said.

"People aren't having fun; you want to jump in and organize games."

"War games," Orne said. "Have you thought of that one?"

"Huh?" Stetson took his gaze off the road momentarily. The buggy swerved, bumped along the road's edge. He jerked his attention back to driving.

"What if some smart R&R type set himself up as emperor on his planet?" Orne asked. "He could start his own dynasty. First thing you'd know about it would be when the bombs started dropping or people started dying from *causes unknown*."

"That's the I-A's personal nightmare," Stetson said. He fell silent.

The sun climbed higher as the ridge road wound on past rocky embankments, far vistas of farmlands, passages of sparse bushes and squat, bulbous trees.

Once, Stetson asked: "What about Hamal's religion?"

"I looked for clues there," Orne said. "They pray to the Overgod of Amel, monotheistic. There was a book of common prayers in the Tritsahin lifeboat. They have a few wandering hermits, but as near as I can make out the hermits are spies for the Council. About three hundred years ago, a holy man began preaching a vision of the Overgod. There's a cult of this visionary now, but no evidence of religious friction."

"Sweetness and light," Stetson said. "A priesthood?"

"Religious leadership stems from the Council. They appoint votaries called 'Keepers of the Prayer.' Nineday cycle of religious observance seems to be the pattern. There's a complex variation on this involving holy days, something called 'Relief Days' and they observe the anniversary of the date when the visionary, name of *Arune,* was transported bodily into heaven. The Priests of Amel have sent a Temporary Dispensation Missive and you can expect the usual conferences, I'm sure, with a subsequent pronouncement proving that the Overgod watches over the least of His creatures."

"Do I detect a note of sarcasm in your voice?" Stetson asked.

"You detect a note of caution," Orne said. "I'm a native of Chargon. Our prophet was Mahmud, who was duly verified by Amel's priesthood. Where Amel is concerned, I walk softly."

"The wise man prays once a week and studies Psi every day," Stetson murmured.

"What?"

"Nothing."

Their road dipped now into a shallow depression between hills, crossed a small brook and slanted up to a new ridge where it swung left along the crest. They could see another village on high ground in the distance. When they were close enough to make out the green and yellow flag atop the government building, Stetson pulled to a stop, opened his window, shut off the engine. The turbine rotor keened downscale to silence. With the window open, the air conditioner off, they felt the oppressive heat of the day.

Sweat began pouring off Orne, settling into a soggy puddle where his bottom touched the seat's plastic depression.

"No aircraft on Hamal?" Stetson asked.

"Not a sign of them."

"Strange."

"Not really. They have a superstition about the

31

dangers of leaving the ground. Result of their narrow escape from space, no doubt. They're just a bit anti-technology—except in the Council where they're more sophisticated about man's toolmaking propensity."

"Black-gang syndrome," Stetson muttered.

"What?"

"Technology is dangerous to sapient creatures," Stetson said. "Lots of cultures and subcultures believe this. There are times when I believe it myself."

"Why've we stopped here?" Orne asked.

"We're waiting."

"For what?"

"For something to happen," Stetson said. "How do the Hamalites feel about peace?"

"They think it's wonderful. The Council is delighted by the peaceful activities of R&R. The common citizenry has a response pattern indicating a rote answer. They say: 'Men find peace in the Overgod.' It's all very consistent."

"Orne, can you tell me why you punched the panic button?" Stetson demanded.

Orne's mouth worked soundlessly, then: "I told you!"

"But what set you off?" Stetson asked. "What straw grounded the blinking rocket?"

Orne swallowed, spoke in a low voice: "A couple of things. For one, they held a banquet to . . ."

"Who held a banquet?"

"The Council. They held a banquet to honor me. And . . . uh . . ."

"They served *froolap*," Stetson said.

"Do you want to hear this or don't you?"

"Dear boy, I'm all ears."

32

Orne glanced pointedly at Stetson's ears, said: "I hadn't noticed." Then: "Well, the Council banquet featured a stew of *porjo* tails that . . ."

"*Porjo?*"

"It's a native rodent. They consider it a delicacy, especially the tails. The Tritsahin castaways survived at first on *porjo.*"

"So they served it at this banquet."

"Right. What they did was—well, the cook, just before bringing me my bowl of stew, tied a live *porjo* with some kind of cord that dissolved quickly in the hot liquid. This animal erupted out of the pot all over me."

"So?"

"They laughed for five minutes. It's the only time I've ever seen Hamalites really laugh."

"You mean they played a practical joke on you and you got mad, so mad you pushed the panic button? I thought you said these people have no sense of humor."

"Look, wise guy! Have you ever stopped to think what kind of people it takes to put a live animal in boiling liquid just to play a joke?"

"A little heavy for humor," Stetson agreed. "But playful all the same. And that's why you called in the I-A?"

"That's part of it!"

"And the rest?"

Orne described the incident of the pratfall into the pile of soft fruit.

"So they just stood there without laughing and this aroused your deepest suspicions," Stetson said.

Orne's face darkened with anger. "So I got mad **at** the *porjo* trick! Go ahead, make something of it! I'm still right about this place! Make something out of that, too!"

"I fully intend to," Setson said. He reached under the go-buggy's instrument panel, pulled out a microphone, spoke into it: "This is Stetson."

So I've really had it, Orne thought. His stomach felt empty and there was a sour taste at the back of his throat.

The humming sound of a space-punch transceiver came from beneath the instrument panel, followed by: "This is the ship. What's doing?" The voice carried the echo flatness of scrambler transmission.

"We have a real baddy here, Hal," Stetson said. "Put out a Priority One emergency call for an occupation force."

Orne jerked upright, stared at the I-A operative.

The transceiver emitted a clanking sound, then: "How bad is it, Stet?"

"One of the worst I've ever seen. Put out a VRO on the First-Contact, some *schlammler* by the name of Bullone. Have him sacked. I don't care if he's Commissioner Bullone's mother! It'd take a blind man, and a stupid one at that, to call Hamal peaceful!"

"Will you have any trouble getting back?" the voice from the speaker asked.

"I doubt it. The R&R operative has been pretty cagey and they probably don't know yet that we're on to them."

"Give me your grid just in case."

Stetson glanced at an indicator on his instrument panel. "A-Eight."

"Gotcha."

"Get that call out immediately, Hal," Stetson said. "I want a full O-force in here by tomorrow!"

"Call's already on its way."

The humming of the space-punch transceiver fell off to silence. Stetson replaced the microphone, turned to Orne. "So you just followed a hunch?"

Orne shook his head. "I . . ."

"Look behind us," Stetson said.

Orne turned, stared back the way they had come.

"See anything curious?" Stetson asked.

Orne fought down a sensation of giddiness, said: "I see a late-coming farmer and one hunter with apprentice moving up fast on the outside."

"I mean the road," Stetson said. "You may consider this a first lesson in I-A technique: a wide road that follows the ridges is a military road. Always. Farm roads are narrow and follow the water level routes. Military roads are wider, avoid swamps and cross rivers at right angles. This one fits all the way."

"But . . ." Orne fell silent as the hunter came up to them, passed their vehicle with only a casual sideglance.

"What's that leather case on his back?" Stetson asked.

"Spyglass."

"Lesson number two," Stetson said. "Telescopes originate as astronomical devices. Spyglasses are developed as an adjunct of a long-range weapon. I would guess those fowling pieces have an effective range of about one hundred meters. *Ergo:* you may take it as proved that they have artillery."

Orne nodded. He still felt dazed with the rapidity of developments, unable as yet to accept complete sensations of relief.

"Now, let's consider that village up ahead," Stetson said. "Notice the flag. Almost inevitably flags originate as banners to follow into battle. Not always. However, you may take this as a good piece of circumstantial evidence in view of the other things."

"I see."

"There's the docility of the civilian populace," Stetson said. "It's axiomatic that this goes hand in glove with a powerful military and/or religious aristocracy which suppresses technological change. Hamal's Leader Council is nothing but an aristocracy, well versed in the use of religion as a tool of statecraft and in the use of spies, another inevitable development occurring with armies and warfare."

"They're aristocrats, all right," Orne agreed.

"Rule one in our book," Stetson said, "says that whenever you have a situation of haves and have-nots, then you have positions to be defended. That always means armies, whether you call them troops or police or guards. I'll bet my bottom credit those gaming fields of the green and yellow balls are disguised drill grounds."

Orne swallowed. "I should've thought of that."

"You did," Stetson said. "Unconsciously. You saw all of the wrongness here unconsciously. It bothered hell out of you. That's why you pushed the panic button."

"I guess you're right."

"Another lesson," Stetson said. "The most important point on the aggression index: peaceful people, really peaceful types, don't even discuss peace. They have developed a dynamic of nonviolence in which the ordinary concept of peace doesn't even occur. They don't even think about it. The only way you develop more than a casual interest in peace as we conceive of it is through the recurrent and violent contrast of war."

"Of course." Orne took a deep breath, stared at the village on the high ground ahead of them. "But what about the lack of forts? I mean, no cavalry animals and . . ."

"We can take it for granted that they have artillery," Stetson said. "Hmmmmm." He rubbed his chin. "Well, that's probably enough. We'll undoubtedly discover a pattern here which rules mobile cavalry out of the equation prohibiting stone forts."

"I guess so."

"What happened here was something like this," Stetson said. "First-Contact, that *schlammler*, may he rot in a military prison, jumped to a wrong conclusion about Hamal. He tipped our hand. The Hamalites got togther, declared a truce, hid or disguised every sign of warfare they knew anything about, put out the word to the citizenry, then concentrated on milking us for everything they could get. Have they sent a deputation to Marak, yet?"

"Yes."

"We'll have to pick them up, too."

"It figures," Orne said. He began to feel the full emotional cleansing of relief, but with odd overtones of disquiet trailing along behind. His own career was out of the soup, but he thought of the consequences for Hamal in what was about to happen. A full O-force! Military occupation did nasty things to the occupiers and the occupied.

"I think you'll make a pretty good I-A operative," Stetson said.

Orne snapped out of his reverie. "I'll make a . . . Huh?"

"I'm drafting you," Stetson said.

Orne stared at him. "Can you do that?"

"There are still a few wise heads in our government," Stetson said. "You may take it for granted that we have this power in the I-A." He scowled. "And we find too damned many of our operatives this way—one step short of disaster."

Orne swallowed. "This is . . ." He fell silent as the farmer pushed his creaking cart past the I-A vehicle.

The men in the go-buggy stared at the peculiar swaying motion of the farmer's back, the solid way his feet came down on the dusty roadbed, the smooth way the high-led vegetable cart rolled along.

"I'm a left-handed *froolap!*" Orne muttered. He pointed at the retreating back. "There's your cavalry animal. That damn wagon's nothing but a chariot!"

Stetson slapped his right fist into his open left palm. "Damn! Right in front of our eyes all the time!" He smiled grimly. "There are going to be some surprised and angry people hereabouts when our O-force arrives tomorrow."

Orne nodded silently, wishing there were some other way to prevent disastrous military excursions into space. And he thought: *What Hamal needs is a new kind of religion, one that shows them how to balance their own lives happily on their world and to balance their world in the universe.*

But with Amel controlling the course of every religion, that was out of the question. There was no such religious balancing system—not on Chargon . . . not even on Marak.

And certainly not on Hamal.

Every sapient creature needs a religion of some kind.

—NOAH ARKWRIGHT
the basic scriptures of Amel

Umbo Stetson paced the landing control bridge of his scout cruiser. His footsteps grated on a floor that was the rear wall of the bridge during flight. Now, the ship rested on its tail fins—all four hundred glistening red and black meters of it. The open ports of the bridge looked out on the jungle roof of the planet Gienah III some one hundred and fifty meters below. A butter-yellow sun hung above the horizon perhaps an hour from setting.

Gienah was a nasty situation and he didn't like using an untested operative in such a place. It concerned him that this particular operative had been drafted into the I-A by a sector chief named Umbo Stetson.

I draft him and I send him out to get killed, Stetson thought. He glanced across the bridge at Lewis Orne, now a junior I-A field operative with a maiden diploma. *Trained . . . and intelligent, but inexperienced.*

"We ought to scrape this planet clean of every living thing on it," Stetson muttered. "Clean as an egg!" He paused in his round of the bridge, glared out the open starboard port into the fire-blackened circle the cruiser had burned from a jungle clearing.

39

The I-A sector chief pulled his head back in the port, stood in his customary slouch. It was a stance not improved by the sacklike patched blue fatigues he wore. Although on this operation he rated the flag of a division admiral, his fatigues carried no insignia. There was a generally unkempt, straggling look about him.

Orne stood at an opposite port, studying the jungle horizon. Something glittered out there too far away to identify; probably the city. Now and then he glanced at the bridge control console, at the chronometer above it, at the big translite map of their position which had been tilted from the upper bulkhead. He felt vaguely uneasy, intensely aware of his heavy-planet muscles overracting on Gienah III with its gravity only seven-eighths Terran Standard. The surgical scars on his neck where the micro-communications equipment had been inserted into his flesh itched maddeningly. He scratched.

"Ha!" Stetson barked. "Politicians!"

A thin black insect with shell-like wings flew in Orne's port, settled in his closely cropped red hair. Orne pulled the insect gently from his hair, released it. Again, it tried to land in his hair. He dodged. The insect flew across the bridge and out the port beside Stetson.

The starchy newness of Orne's blue I-A fatigues failed to conceal his no-fat appearance. It gave Orne a look of military spit and polish, but something about his blocky, off-center features suggested the clown.

"I'm getting tired of waiting," Orne said.

"*You're* tired! Ha!"

"You hear anything new from Hamal?" Orne asked.

"Forget Hamal! Concentrate on Gienah!"

"I was just curious, trying to pass the time."

A breeze rippled the tops of the green ocean below them. Here and there, red and purple flowers jutted from the verdure, bending and nodding like an attentive audience. The rich odor of rotting and growing vegetation came in the open ports.

"Just look at that blasted jungle!" Stetson said. "Them and their stupid orders!"

Orne listened quietly to the sounds of anger from his chief. Gienah obviously was a *very* special, *very* dangerous problem. Orne's thoughts, though, kept going back to Hamal. The O-force had taken over on that planet and things were in their expected mess. No way had ever been found to keep occupying troops from betraying an overbearing attitude and engaging in certain oppressive activities—such as picking off all the prettiest and most willing women. When the O-force finally lifted from Hamal, the people of that planet might be peaceful, but they'd bear scars which five hundred generations might not erase.

A call bell tinkled on the bridge console above Orne. The red light at the speaker grid began blinking. Stetson shot an angry glance at the offending equipment. "Yeah, Hal?"

"Okay, Stet. Orders just came through. We use Plan C. ComGo says you may now brief the fieldman on the classified information, then jet the aitch out of here."

"Did you ask them about using another fieldman?"

Orne looked up attentively. Secrecy piled upon secrecy and now this?

"Negative. It's crash priority. ComGo expects to blast the planet anyway."

Stetson glared at the speaker grid. "Those fat-headed, lard-bottomed, pig-brained, schlemmel-hearted POLITICIANS!" He took two deep breaths. "Okay. Tell them we'll comply."

"Confirmation's on the way. You want me to come up and help in the briefing?"

"No. I . . . Dammit! Ask them again if I can take this one!"

"Stet, they said we have to use Orne because of the records on the Delphinus."

Stetson sighed, then: "Will they give us more time to brief him?"

"Crash priority, Stet. We're wasting time."

"If it isn't one . . ."

"Stet!"

"What now?"

"I just got a confirmed contact."

Stetson brought himself upright, poised on the balls of his feet. "Where?"

Orne glanced out the port, returned his attention to Stetson. The electric feeling of urgency and reluctance in the bridge made his stomach churn.

"Contact . . . about ten klicks out," the speaker rasped.

"How many?"

"A mob. You want I should count them?"

"No. What're they doing?"

"Making a beeline for us. You'd better move it."

"Right. Keep us posted.

"Wilco."

Stetson looked across at his untried junior fieldman. "Orne, if you decide you want out of this assignment, you just say the word. I'll back you to the limit."

"Why should I want out of my first assignment?"

"Listen, and find out." Stetson crossed to a tilt-

42

locker beside the big translite map, hauled out a white coverall uniform with gold insignia, tossed it to Orne. "Get into these while I brief you."

"But this is an R&R uni—"

"Get that damn uniform on your ugly frame!"

"Yes, sir, Admiral Stetson, sir. Right away, sir. But I thought I was through with old Rediscovery & Reeducation when you drafted me into the I-A." He began changing from the I-A blue into the R&R white. Almost as an afterthought, he said: ". . . sir."

A wolfish grin cracked Stetson's big features. "You know, Orne, one of the reasons I drafted you was your proper attitude of subservience toward authority."

Orne sealed the long seam of the coverall uniform. "Oh, yes, *sir* . . . sir."

"All right, knock it off and pay attention." Stetson gestured at the translite map with its green superimposed grid. "Here we are." He put a finger on the map. "Here's that city we flew over on our way down." The finger moved. "You'll head for the city as soon as we drop you. The city's big enough that if you hold a course roughly northeast you can't miss it. We're . . ."

Again the call bell rang, the light flashed.

"What is it this time, Hal?" Stetson barked.

"They've changed to Plan H, Stet. New orders cut."

"Five days?"

"That's all they can give us."

"Holy . . ."

"ComGo says we can't keep the information out of High Commissioner Bullone's hands any longer than that."

"It's five days then," Stetson sighed.

Orne moved closer to the map, asked: "Is it the usual R&R foul-up?"

43

Stetson grimaced. "Worse, thanks to Bullone and company. We're just one jump ahead of another catastrophe, but they still pump the Rah & Rah into the boys back at dear old Uni-Galacta."

"It's either go out and rediscover the lost planets or let them rediscover us," Orne said. "I prefer the former."

"Yeah, and we're going to rediscover one too many someday, but this Gienah is a different breed of fish. It's not, repeat *not,* a *re*discovery."

Orne felt his muscles stiffen. "Alien?"

"A-L-I-E-N," Stetson spelled it out. "A species and a culture we've never before contacted. That language you were force-fed on the way out here, that's an alien language. It's not complete, but all we have off the *minis.* And we didn't give you the basic data, what little we have, on the natives, because we've been hoping to scrub this place and nobody the wiser."

"Holy mazoo! Why?"

"Twenty-six days ago an I-A sector searcher came on this planet, made a routine mini-sneaker survey. When he combed in his net of sneakers to check their data, lo and behold he had a little stranger."

"One of *theirs?*"

"No, one of ours. It was a *mini* off the Delphinus Rediscovery. The Delphinus has been unreported for eighteen standard months. Cause of disappearance unknown."

"You think it cracked up here."

"We don't know. If it did crash on Gienah, we haven't been able to spot it. And we've looked, son. Believe me, we've looked. And now we've something else on our minds. It's the one little item that makes me want to blot Gienah and run home with my tail be-

44

tween my legs. We've a . . ."

Again the call bell chimed.

"NOW WHAT?" Stetson roared.

"I've sneaked a *mini* over that mob, Stet. They're talking about us, near as I can make out. It looks like a definite raiding party and armed."

"What armament?"

"Too gloomy down there to be absolutely certain. The infra beam's not working on this *mini*. They look like hard pellet rifles of some kind, though. Might even be off the Delphinus."

"Can you get closer to make sure?"

"No sense risking it without the infra. Light's very poor down there. They're moving up fast, though."

"Keep an eye on them, but don't ignore the other sectors," Stetson said.

"You think I was born yesterday?" The voice from the speaker was an angry rasping. The sound bapped off with a curt abruptness.

"One thing I like about the I-A," Stetson said. "It collects such even-tempered types." He stared gloomily at the white uniform on Orne, wiped a hand across his mouth as though he'd tasted something dirty.

"Why *am* I wearing this thing?" Orne asked.

"Disguise."

"But where's the mustache to go with it?"

Stetson smiled without humor. "I-A is developing its own answer to these fat-keistered politicians. We're setting up our own search system; find the planets before *they* do. We've managed to put spies in key places at R&R. Any touchy planets our spies report, we divert the files."

"Oh."

"Then we look into said planets with bright boys such as yourself . . . disguised as R&R."

"Goody. And what happens if R&R stumbles onto me while I'm down there playing patty-cake with the aliens?"

"We disown you."

"Nuts! They'd never. . . . Hey! You said an I-A ship found this place."

"It did. Then one of our spies in R&R intercepted a *routine* request for an agent-instructor to be assigned here with full equipment. Request signed by a First-Contact officer name of Riso . . . off the Delphinus!"

"But the . . ."

"Yeah, missing. The routine request was a forgery. And now you see why I'm for rubbing this place. Who'd dare forge such a request unless he knew for sure the original F-C officer was missing . . . or dead?"

"Stet, what the jumped-up mazoo are we doing here?" Orne demanded. "Alien contact calls for a full team of experts with all the . . ."

"This one calls for one planet-buster bomb, buster. In five days. Unless you give them a white bill in the meantime. High Commissioner Bullone will have word of this planet by then. If Gienah still exists in five days, can you imagine the fun the politicians'll have with it? Oh, Mamma! Orne, we want this planet cleared for contact or dead before then."

"We're allowing ourselves to be stampeded," Orne said. "I don't like this. Look at what happened on . . ."

"YOU don't like it!"

"There has to be another way, Stet. When we teamed up with the Alerinoids we gained five hundred years in the physical sciences alone, not to mention the . . ."

46

"The Alerinoids didn't knock over one of our survey ships."

"But what if the Delphinus crashed here? That's a big jungle. If the locals just stumbled onto . . ."

"That's what you're going to find out, Orne. I hope. You're going to be the answer to their *routine* request, an R&R agent-instructor. But answer me this, Mister R&R, how long before a tool-using species could be a threat to the Galaxy—given the information that's in your head?"

"You saw that city, the size of it. They could be dug in within six months and there'd be no . . ."

"Yeah."

Orne shook his head. "But think of it: two civilizations that matured along different lines. Think of all the different ways we'd approach similar problems, the lever that'd give us for . . ."

"You sound like a Uni-Galacta lecture. Are you through marching arm and arm into the misty future?"

Orne took a deep breath. He felt that he was being pushed too fast to make rational decisions. He asked: "Why me? You're tossing me into this. Why?"

"The Delphinus master lists. You'd still be on 'em as an R&R fieldman, full identification, eye pattern, everything. That's important if you're masquerading as . . ."

"Am I the only one you have? I'm a recent convert to I-A, but . . ."

"You want out?"

"I didn't say that. I just want to know why I'm . . ."

"Because the bigdomes at HQ fed a set of requirements into one of their mechanical monsters. Your name popped out. They were looking for somebody capable, dependable . . . and expendable."

"Hey!"

"That's why I'm down here briefing you instead of sitting back on a flagship. *I* got you into the I-A. Now, you listen carefully: If you push the panic button here without cause I will personally flay you. We both know the advantages of an alien contact. But if you get into a really hot spot and call for help, I'll dive this cruiser into that city to get you out. Clear?"

Orne tried to swallow in a dry throat. "Yes. And thanks, Stet, but if . . ."

"We'll take up a tight orbit. Out beyond us will be five transports full of I-A marines plus a Class IX Monitor with one planet-buster. You're calling the shots, God help you! First, we have to know if they've taken the Delphinus, and if so, where it is. Next, we want to know how warlike these goons are. Can we deal with them? Are they too bloodthirsty? What's their potential?"

"In five days?"

"Not a second more."

"What do we know about them?"

"Not much. They look something like an ancient Terran chimpanzee, but with blue fur. Face is hairless, pink-skinned." Stetson touched a button at his waist. The translite map above him became a screen with a figure frozen on it. "This is life size."

"Looks like the famous missing link," Orne said.

"Yeah, but you've a different kind of link to find."

"Vertical slit pupil in their eyes," Orne said. He studied the figure intently. The Gienahn had been recorded from the front by a mini-sneaker. The figure stood about a meter and a half tall. The stance was slightly bent forward, long arms hanging. The nose

48

was flat with two vertical slits. The mouth was a lipless gash above a receding chin. Four fingers on the hands. It wore a wide belt from which dangled neat pouches and what appeared to be tools, although their use was obscure. Perhaps they were weapons. There appeared to be the tip of a tail protruding from behind one of the squat legs.

The creature stood on lawn like greenery and behind it towered the faery spires of the city they'd observed from the air.

"Tails?" Orne asked.

"Right. They're arboreal. Not a road on the whole planet that we can find. Lots of vine lanes through the jungle, though." Stetson's face hardened. "Match *that* with a city as advanced as the one there."

"Slave culture?"

"Probably."

"How many cities do they have?"

"We've found two. This one and another on the far side. The other one's a ruin."

"War?"

"You tell us. Lots of mysteries here."

"How extensive is the jungle cover?"

"Almost complete on the land surfaces. There are polar oceans, a few lakes and rivers. One low mountain chain follows the equatorial belt about two-thirds of the way around the planet. Continental drift scars are old. The surface has been stabilized for a long time."

"And only two cities. Are you sure of that?"

"Reasonably. It'd be pretty hard to miss something the size of that place." He pointed to the city behind the figure on the screen. "It must be two hundred kilometers long, at least fifty wide. It's swarming with these creatures. We've a good zone-count estimate; it places this city's population at more than thirty million. In population, it's the biggest single city we've ever heard of."

"Whee-ew," Orne breathed. "Look at the size of those buildings. What these Gienahns could tell us about urban living."

"And we may never hear what they have to say, Orne. Unless you bring them into the fold, there'll be nothing but ashes for our archaeologists to pick over."

"There *has* to be some other way!"

"I agree, but . . ."

The call bell jingled.

Stetson's voice sounded tired: "Yeah, Hal?"

"That mob's only about five klicks out, Stet. Orne's gear is outside in the disguised air sled."

"We'll be right down."

"Why a disguised sled?" Orne asked.

"Hal's idea. If the Gienahns think it's a ground buggy, they may get careless when you most need an advantage. We could always scoop you out of the air, you know."

"Stet, what're my chances?"

"Slim. Maybe less than that. These goons probably captured the Delphinus. Our best guess is they want you just long enough to get your equipment and everything you know."

"Only five days?"

"If you're not out by then, we blast."

"Expendable."

"You want to turn down this mission?"

"No."

"Didn't expect you to. Look, use the back-door rule, son. Always leave yourself a way out."

50

"The way you're doing," Orne said.

Stetson stared at him for several heartbeats, then: "Yeah. Let's check that equipment the surgeons put in your neck."

"I was wondering about that."

Stetson put a hand to his own throat. His mouth remained closed, but a surf-hissing voice became audible to Orne, radiating from the implanted transceiver: "You read me, Orne?"

"I read you. Is this . . ."

"No!" the voice hissed. "Touch the mike contact. Keep your mouth closed. Just use your speaking muscles without speaking aloud."

Orne obeyed, hand to throat. "How's this?"

"That's better," Stetson said. "You come in loud and clear."

"How far will this transmit?"

"There'll be a relay sneaker close to you at all times," Stetson said. "Now, when you're not touching the mike contact, this rig will still feed us everything you say and everything that goes on around you. We'll monitor everything. Got that?"

"I hope so."

Stetson held out his right hand. "Good luck, Orne. I meant that about diving in for you. Just say the word."

"I know the word," Orne said. "It's HELP!"

Bow down to Ullua, the star wanderer of the
Ayrbs. Let no blasphemy occur, nor permit a blas-
phemer to live. May blasphemy shrivel the mouth.
Blasphemers are accursed of God and accursed of
the blessed. Let this curse strike a blasphemer from
the sole of his foot to the crown of his head, sleeping
and waking, sitting and standing . . .

—Invocation for the Day of Bairam

Gray mud floor and gloomy aisles between monstrous blue tree trunks—that was the Gienah jungle. Only the weakest glimmering of sunlight penetrated to the mud.

Orne's disguised sled, its paragrav units turned off, lurched and skidded around buttress roots. The headlights swung in wild arcs across the trunks and down to the mud. Aerial creepers, great looping vines of them, swung down from the towering forest ceiling. A steady drip of condensation spattered the windshield, forcing Orne to use screen blowers.

In the bucket seat of the sled's cab, Orne fought the controls while trying to watch on all sides for sign of the Gienahn raiding party. He felt plagued by the vague slow-motion-floating sensations a heavy planet native always experienced in lighter gravity. It gave him an unhappy stomach.

Things skipped through the air around the lurching vehicle—flitting and darting things, blue, red, green, violet, iridescent and dull things. Gienahn insects with fuzzy wings came in twin cones, siphoned toward the headlights. An endless chittering screeching whistling

52

chiming tok-tok-toking sounded in the gloom beyond the sled's lights.

Stetson's voice hissed suddenly through Orne's surgically implanted speaker: "How's it look?"

"Alien."

"Any sign of that mob?"

"Negative."

"Right. We're taking off. Good luck."

From behind Orne, there came the deep rumbling roar of the scout cruiser climbing its jets. The racket receded. All other sounds hung suspended in after-silence, then resumed: the strongest first and then the weaker.

A heavy dark object arced through the headlights, swinging on a vine. It disappeared behind a tree. Another. Another. Ghostly shadows on vine pendulums looped across both sides of the sled. Something banged down heavily on the hood.

Orne braked to a creaking stop that shifted the load behind him. He found himself staring through the windshield at a native of Gienah. The native crouched on the hood, a Mark XX exploding-pellet rifle in his right hand directed at Orne's head. In the abrupt shock of meeting, Orne recognized the weapon: standard issue to marine guards on all R&R survey ships.

The native appeared the twin of the one Orne had seen on the translite screen, even to the belt with its pouched artifacts. The four-fingered hand looked practiced and capable around the stock of the Mark XX.

Slowly, Orne put a hand to his throat, activated the hidden microphone, moved his speaking muscles:

"*Just made contact. One of that mob's on the hood now. He has one of our Mark XX rifles aimed at my head.*"

The surf-hissing of Stetson's voice came through the implanted speaker: "*Want us back?*"

"*Negative. Stand by. He looks more curious than hostile.*"

"*Be careful. You can't be sure of reactions in an unknown species.*"

Orne took his right hand from his neck, held it up, the palm out. He had a second thought, held up his left hand, too. Universal symbol of peaceful intentions: empty hands. The rifle muzzle lowered slightly. Orne called to mind the Gienahn language that had been hypno-forced into him. *Ocheero? No, that meant "The People." Ahh* . . . And he recalled the heavy fricative greeting sound.

"Ffroiragrazzi," he said.

The native shifted to the left, answered in pure, unaccented high Galactese: "Who are you?"

Orne fought down sudden panic. The lipless mouth had appeared so odd forming the familiar words.

Stetson's voice hissed: "*Was that the native speaking Galactese?*"

Orne touched his throat: "*You heard him.*"

"Who are you?" the Gienahn demanded.

Orne dropped his hand, said: "I'm Lewis Orne of the Rediscovery and Reeducation Service. I was sent here at the request of the First-Contact officer on the Delphinus Rediscovery."

"Where is your ship?" the Gienahn demanded.

"It put me down and left."

"Why?"

"It was behind schedule for another appointment."

Out of the corners of his eyes, Orne saw more shadows drop to the mud around him. The sled shifted as someone climbed onto the load behind the cab.

The native climbed down to the sled's side step, slid the door open in one slamming motion. The rifle remained at the ready. Again, the lipless mouth formed Galactese: "What do you carry in your . . . vehicle?"

"The R&R equipment, the things a fieldman requires to help the people of a rediscovered planet restore their civilization and economy." Orne nodded at the rifle. "Would you mind pointing that weapon some other direction? It makes me nervous."

The gun muzzle remained unwaveringly on Orne's middle. The Gienahn's mouth opened, revealing long canines and a blue tongue. "Do we not look strange to you?"

"I take it there's been a heavy mutational variation in the humanoid norm on this planet," Orne said. "What was it? Hard radiation?"

The Gienahn remained silent.

Orne said: "It doesn't really make any difference. I'm here to help you as we do with all rediscovered planets."

"I am Tanub, High Path Chief of the Grazzi," the native said. "I decide who is to help."

Orne swallowed.

"Where do you go?" Tanub demanded.

"I was headed toward your city. Is that permitted?"

Tanub remained silent for several heartbeats while his vertical-slit pupils expanded and contracted. The eyes reminded Orne of a great feline deciding whether to leap.

Presently, Tanub said: "It is permitted."

Stetson's voice hissed through the hidden speaker:

"All bets off, Orne! We're coming in after you. Galactese plus that Mark XX, this is a new game. They have the Delphinus for sure."

Orne touched his throat. *"No! Give me a little more time."*

"Why?"

"You'd put me right in the middle of a fire fight! Besides, I have a hunch about these Gienahns."

"What is it?"

"No time now. Trust me."

There was a long pause in which Orne and Tanub continued to study each other. Presently, Stetson said: *"Very well. Go ahead as planned. But find out where they've hidden the Delphinus. If we get our ship back, we pull some of their teeth."*

"Why do you keep touching yourself?" Tanub asked.

Orne took his hand from his throat. "I'm nervous. Guns always make me nervous."

Tanub lowered the muzzle slightly.

"Shall we continue on to your city?" Orne asked. He wet his lips with his tongue. The green cab light gave the Gienahn's face an eerie sinister appearance.

"We can go soon," Tanub said.

"Will you join me inside here?" Orne asked. "There's a passenger seat right behind me."

Tanub's gaze moved catlike, right, left. "Yes." He turned, barked an order into the jungle gloom, then climbed in behind Orne.

There was a wet fur odor with a touch of acid in it about the Gienahn.

"When do we go?" Orne asked.

"The great sun goes down soon," Tanub said. "We can continue as soon as *Chiranachuruso* rises."

"Chiranachuruso?"

"Our satellite . . . our moon."

"What a beautiful word," Orne said. *"Chiranachuruso."*

"In our tongue it means 'The Limb of Victory,' " Tanub said. "By its light we will continue."

Orne turned, looked back at Tanub. "Do you mean to tell me you can see by what light gets down here through those trees?"

"Can you not see?" Tanub asked.

"Not without the headlights."

"Our eyes differ," Tanub said. He bent toward Orne, peered at Orne's eyes. The Gienahn's vertical slit pupils expanded, contracted. "You are the same as the . . . others."

"Oh, on the Delphinus?"

"Yes."

Orne forced himself to fall silent then. He wanted to ask about the Delphinus, but sensed how narrow a path of tolerance he walked. They knew so little about the Gienahns. How did they reproduce? What was their religion? It was obvious that Stetson and the brass behind him didn't expect this mission to succeed. This was a desperation move with an expendable pawn.

A sudden feeling of sympathy for the Gienahns came over Orne. Tanub and his fellows had no say in their own fate. Desperate humans were calling all of the moves.

Desperate and frightened humans who had grown up in the shadow of the Rim War terrors. Did that give these humans the right to decide whether an entire species should survive? These Gienahns were sapient creatures.

57

Although he had never considered himself very religious, Orne said a silent prayer: "Mahmud, help me save these . . . people."

An inner calmness washed all through him, a sensation of strength and confidence. He thought: *I'm calling the moves!*

A cool gloom swept over the jungle, bringing a sudden stillness to the wild sounds. A chittering commotion came from the Gienahns in the trees and around the sled.

Tanub shifted, grunted.

The Gienahn who had been standing atop the load jumped down to the left.

"We go now," Tanub said. "Slowly. Stay behind my . . . scouts."

"Right." Orne eased the sled forward around an obstructing root, watched the headlights pick up the swinging, scampering figures of his escort.

Silence invaded the cab while they crawled forward.

"Turn a little to your right," Tanub said, indicating an aisle between the trees.

Orne obeyed. Around him shapes flung themselves from vine to vine.

"I admired your city from the air," Orne said. "It is very beautiful."

"Yes," Tanub said. "Your kind finds it so. Why did you bring your ship down so far from our city?"

"We didn't want to land where we might destroy anything."

"There is nothing to destroy in the jungle, Orne."

"Why do you have just the one big city?" Orne asked.

Silence.

"I said, why do you . . ."

"Orne, you are ignorant of our ways," Tanub growled. "Therefore, I forgive you. The city is for our race, for the foreverness. Our young must be born in sunlight. Once, long ago, we used crude platforms on the tops of the trees. Now . . . only the wild ones do this."

Stetson's voice hissed in Orne's ears: *"Easy on the sex and breeding line. That's always touchy. These creatures are oviparous. Sex glands apparently are hidden in that long fur behind where their chins ought to be."*

Who decides where chins ought to be? Orne wondered.

"The ones who control the birthing sites control our world," Tanub said. "Once there was another city. We destroyed it, shattered its towers and sent it crashing into the dirty mud where the jungle can reclaim it."

"Are there many . . . wild ones?" Orne asked.

"Fewer each season," Tanub said. His voice sounded boastful, confident.

"There's how they get their slaves," Stetson said.

"Soon, there will be no wild ones left," Tanub said.

"You speak excellent Galactese," Orne said.

"The High Path Chief commands the best teacher," Tanub said. "Do you, too, know many things, Orne?"

"That's why I was sent here," Orne said.

"Are there many planets to teach?" Tanub asked.

"Very many," Orne said. "Your city—I saw very tall buildings. Of what do you build them?"

"In your tongue, *glass*," Tanub said. "The engineers of the Delphinus said it was impossible. As you saw, they are wrong."

Stetson's voice came hissing on the carrier wave:

"A glassblowing culture! That'd explain a lot of things."

The disguised air sled crept down the jungle aisle as Orne reviewed what he had heard and what he had observed. Glassblowers. High Path Chief. Eyes with vertical slit pupils. An arboreal species. Hunters. Warlike. Slave culture. The young must be born in sunlight. Culture? Or physical necessity? They learned quickly. They'd had the Delphinus and her crew only eighteen standard months.

A scout swooped down into the headlights, waved.

Orne stopped the sled on Tanub's order. They waited almost ten minutes before proceeding.

"Wild ones?" Orne asked.

"Perhaps. But we are too strong a force for them to attack. And they do not have good weapons. Do not be afraid, Orne."

A glowing of many lights grew visible through the giant tree trunks. It brightened as the sled crept through the jungle's edge and emerged in cleared land looking across about two kilometers of open space at the city.

Orne stared upward in awe. The Gienahn city fluted and spiraled into the moonlit sky, taller than the tallest trees. It appeared a fragile lacery of bridges, glowing columns and winking dots of light. The bridges wove back and forth from column to column until the entire visible network seemed one gigantic dew-glittering web.

"All that with glass," Orne murmured.

"What's happening?" Stetson demanded.

Orne touched his throat: *"We're just out of the jungle and proceeding toward the nearest buildings of the city. They are magnificent!"*

"Too bad if we have to blast the place."

Orne thought of a Chargonian curse: *May you grow like a wild root with your head in the ground!*

Tanub said: "This is far enough, Orne. Stop your vehicle."

Orne brought the sled to a jolting stop. He could see armed Gienahns all around in the moonlight—Mark XX's, hand blasters. The glass-buttressed pedestal of a columnar building lifted into the moonlight directly ahead. It appeared taller than had the scout cruiser in the jungle landing circle.

Tanub leaned over Orne's shoulder. "We have not deceived you, Orne, have we?"

Orne felt his stomach contract. "What do you mean?" The furry odor of the Gienahn was oppressive in the cab.

"You have recognized that we cannot be mutated members of your race," Tanub said.

Orne tried to swallow in a dry throat. Stetson's voice came into his ears: *"Better admit it."*

"That's true," Orne said.

"I like you, Orne," Tanub said. "You shall be one of my slaves. I will give you fine females from the Delphinus and you will teach me many things."

"How did you capture the Delphinus?" Orne asked.

"How do you know of this?" Tanub drew back and Orne saw the rifle muzzle come up.

"You have one of their rifles," Orne said. "We don't pass around weapons. Our aim is to reduce the numbers of weapons throughout the . . ."

"Weak ground crawlers!" Tanub said. "You are no match for us, Orne. We take the high path. Our prowess is great. We surpass all other creatures in cunning. We shall subjugate you."

"How'd you take the Delphinus?" Orne asked.

"Ha! They brought their ship into our reach because it had inferior tubes. We told them truthfully that we could improve their tubes. Very inferior ceramics your kind makes."

Orne studied Tanub in the dim glow of the cab light. "Tanub, have you heard of the I-A?"

"I-A! They investigate and adjust when others make mistakes. Their existence is an admission of your inferiority. You make mistakes!"

"Many people make mistakes," Orne said.

A wary tenseness came over the Gienahn. His mouth opened to reveal the long canines.

"You took the Delphinus by treachery?" Orne asked.

Stetson's voice came hissing on the carrier wave into Orne's hearing: *"Don't goad him!"*

Tanub said: "They were simple fools on the Delphinus. We are smaller than your kind; they thought us weaker." The Mark XX's muzzle came around to center on Orne's stomach. "You will answer a question. Why do you speak of this I-A?"

"I am of the I-A," Orne said. "I came here to find out where you'd hidden the Delphinus."

"You came to die," Tanub said. "We have hidden your ship in the place that suits us best. In all of our history there has never been a better place for us to crouch and await the moment of attack."

"You see no alternative to attack?" Orne asked.

"In the jungle, the strong slay the weak until only the strong remain," Tanub said.

"Then the strong prey upon each other," Orne said.

62

"That is a quibble for weaklings!"

"Or for those who have seen this kind of thinking make entire worlds uninhabitable for any form of life—nothing left for the strong or the weak."

"Within one of your years, Orne, we will be ready. Then we shall see which of us is correct."

"It's too bad you feel that way," Orne said. "When two cultures meet as ours are meeting they tend to help each other. Each gains. What have you done with the crew from the Delphinus?"

"They are slaves," Tanub said. "Those of them who still live. Some resisted. Others objected to teaching us what it is we must know." He pointed the Mark XX at Orne's head. "You will not be foolish enough to object, will you, Orne?"

"No need for me to be foolish," Orne said. "We of the I-A are also teachers. We teach lessons to people who make mistakes. You have made a mistake, Tanub. You have told me where you have hidden the Delphinus."

"Go, boy!" Stetson shouted on the hissing carrier wave. *"Where is it?"*

"Impossible!" Tanub snarled. The gun muzzle remained centered on Orne's head.

"It's on your moon," Orne said. "Dark side. It's on a mountain on the dark side of your moon."

Tanub's eyes dilated, contracted. "You read minds?"

"No need for the I-A to read minds," Orne said. "We rely on superior mental prowess and the mistakes of others."

"Two attack monitors are on their way," Stetson's voice hissed. *"We're coming in to get you. I'll want to know how you figured this one out."*

"You are a weak fool like the others," Tanub gritted.

"It's too bad you formed your opinion of us by observing the low grades of R&R," Orne said.

"Easy, easy," Stetson cautioned. *"Don't pick a fight now. Remember he's arboreal, probably as strong as an ape."*

"You ground-crawling slave," Tanub grated. "I could kill you where you sit."

"You kill your entire planet if you do," Orne said. "I'm not alone, Tanub. Others listen to every word we say. There's a ship above us that could split open your planet with one bomb—wash everything with molten rock. Your planet would run like the glass of your buildings. Your entire planet would be one big piece of ceramic."

"You lie!"

"I'll make you an offer," Orne said. "We don't want to exterminate you. We won't unless you force our hand. We'll give you limited membership in the Galactic Federation until you've proven you're no menace to other . . ."

"You dare insult me," Tanub growled.

"You'd better believe me," Orne said. "We—"

Stetson's voice interrupted: *"Got it, Orne! They caught the Delphinus in a tight little mountain valley right where you said it'd be! Blew the tubes off it. We're mopping up now."*

"It's like this, Tanub," Orne said. "We've already recaptured the Delphinus."

Tanub's gaze darted skyward. He returned his attention to Orne. "Impossible. We have your communications equipment and there has been no signal. The lights of our city still glow and you will not . . ."

"You've only the inferior R&R equipment," Orne said, "not what we use in the I-A. Your people kept silent up there until it was too late. It's their way, not that . . ."

Stetson demanded: *"How'd you know that?"*

Orne ignored Stetson, said: "Except for the captured armament you still hold, you obviously don't have the weapons to meet us, Tanub. Otherwise you wouldn't be carrying that rifle off the Delphinus."

"If this is truth, then we shall die bravely," Tanub said.

"No need," Orne said. "We don't . . ."

"I cannot take the chance that you lie," Tanub said. "I must kill you."

Orne's foot on the air sled control pedal kicked downward. The sled shot upward, heavy G's pressing its occupants into their seats. The gun was slammed into Tanub's lap. He struggled to raise it.

For Orne, the weight still remained only about twice that of his native Chargon. He reached over, removed the rifle from Tanub's grasp, found safety belts, bound the Gienahn with them. Then Orne eased off on the acceleration.

Tanub stared at him in teeth-bared fear.

"We don't need slaves," Orne said. "We have machines to do most of our work. We'll send experts in here, teach you how to get into better balance with your planet, how to build good transportation, how to mine your minerals, how to . . ."

"And what do we do in return?" Tanub whispered. He appeared cowed by Orne's strength.

"You could start by teaching us to make superior ceramics," Orne said. As he spoke, a series of formative thoughts fled through his awareness—the peace-keeping function of the marketplace, the deliberate despecialization of manufacture with one village making the head of the hoe and the next village making the handle, the psychological security of guilds and castes . . .

Almost as an afterthought, he said: "I hope you see things our way. We truly don't want to have to come down here and clean you out—although now we see that we could. But it'd be profoundly disturbing to us if we had to blast your city and send you back into the jungle for places to bear your young."

Tanub wilted. "The city," he whispered. Presently, he said: "Send me to my people. I will discuss what I have learned with . . . our . . . council." He stared at Orne and there was respect in his manner. "You I-A's are too strong . . . too strong. We did not suspect this."

Because the earliest Psi sensations came upon mankind from the unknown, primitive emotional associations with Psi were those of fear and the maya projection of false realities, of incubi and witches and warlocks and sabbats. These associations are bred into us and our kind has a strong tendency to recapitulate the old mistakes.

—HALMYRACH, ABBOD OF AMEL,
Psi and Religion

In the wardroom of Stetson's scout cruiser, the lights were low, the chairs comfortable and close to a green-beige table set with crystalate glasses and a decanter of dark Hochar brandy.

Orne lifted his glass, sipped the liquor. He said: "For a while there I thought I'd never again be tasting anything as lovely as this."

Stetson poured a glass of the brandy for himself, said: "ComGo heard the whole thing over the monitor net. D'you know you've been breveted to senior fieldman?"

"They've recognized my sterling worth at last," Orne said. As he spoke, he found the bantering lightness of his own words disturbing. He tried to recapture an elusive memory—something about primitive gardening, about tools . . .

A wolfish grin spread over Stetson's big features. "Senior fieldmen last about half as long as the juniors," he said. "Very high mortality."

"I might've known," Orne said. He took another sip of the brandy, his thoughts going to the fate of the Gienahns, of the Hamalites: military occupation. Call it I-A necessity, call it preventative surveillance—it still spelled control-by-force.

Stetson flicked the switch of his cruiser's master recorder system, said: "Let's get it on record."

"Where do you want me to start?"

"Who authorized you to offer the Gienahns limited membership in the Galactic Federation?"

"It seemed like a good idea at the time."

"But junior fieldmen do not originate such offers."

"ComGo objects?"

"ComGo was telling me to authorize it when you jumped the gun. They weren't on your net, were they?"

"No . . . no, they weren't."

"Tell me, Orne, how'd you tumble to where they'd hidden the Delphinus? We'd already made a quick scan of the moon and it didn't seem possible they'd try to hide it up there."

"It had to be there. Tanub's word for his people was *Grazzi*. Most sentients call themselves something meaning 'The People.' But in his tongue, that's *Ocheero*. There was no such word as *Grazzi* on our translation list. I started working on it. There had to be a conceptual superstructure here with direct relationship to the animal shape, to the animal characteristics—just as there is with us. I felt that if I could get at the conceptual models for their communication, I had them. I was working under life-and-death pressure and, strangely, it was their lives and their deaths that concerned me."

"Yes, yes, get on with it," Stetson said.

"One step at a time," Orne chided. "But on solid ground. By that time, I knew quite a bit about the

Gienahns. They had wild enemies in the jungle, creatures much like themselves who lived in what might be enviable freedom. *Grazzi. Grazzi.* I wondered if it might not be a word adopted from another language. What if it meant 'enemy'?"

"I don't see where this is leading," Stetson said.

"It is leading us to the Delphinus."

"That . . . that *word* told you where the Delphinus was?"

"No, but it fitted the creature pattern of the Gienahns. I'd felt from our first contact that the Gienahns might have a culture similar to that of the Indians on ancient Terra."

"You mean with castes and devil worship, that sort of thing?"

"Not those Indians. The Amerinds, the aborigines of wilderness America."

"What made you suspect this?"

"They came at me like a primitive raiding party. The leader dropped right onto the rotor hood of my sled. It was an act of bravery, nothing less than counting coup."

"Counting what?"

"Challenging me in a way that put the challenger in immediate peril. Making me look silly."

"I'm not tracking on this, Orne."

"Be patient; we'll get there."

"To how you learned where they'd secreted the Delphinus?"

"Of course. You see, this leader, this Tanub identified himself immediately as High Path Chief. That wasn't on our translation list either. But it was easy: *Raider Chief.* There's a word in almost every language

69

in our history to mean 'raider' and deriving from a word for road or path or highway."

"Highwayman," Stetson said.

" 'Raid' itself," Orne said. "It's a corruption of an ancient human word for road."

"Yeah, yeah, but where'd all this . . ."

"We're almost home, Stet. Now, what'd we know about them at this point? Glassblowing culture. Everything pointed to the assumption that they were recently emerged from the primitive. They played into our hands then by telling us how vulnerable their species survival was—dependent upon the high city in the sunlight."

"Yeah, we got that up here. It meant we could control them."

"Control's a bad word, Stet. But we'll skip it for now. You want to know about the clues in their animal shape, their language and all the rest of it. Very well: Tanub said their moon was *Chiranachuruso*. Translation: 'The Limb of Victory.' When I had that, it all fell into place."

"I don't see how."

"The vertical slit pupils of their eyes."

"What's that mean?"

"It means night-hunting predator accustomed to dropping upon its prey from above. No other type of creature has ever had the vertical slit in its light sensors. And Tanub said the Delphinus was hidden in the best place in all of their history. For that to track, the hiding place had to be somewhere high, very high. Likewise, dark. Put it together: a high place on the dark side of *Chiranachuruso*, on 'The Limb of Victory.' "

"I'm a pie-eyed greepus," Stetson whispered.

Orne grinned at him. "I won't agree with you . . . sir. The way I feel right now, if I said it, you might turn into a greepus. I've had enough nonhuman associates for a while."

"It is by death that life is known," the Abbod said. *"Without the eternal presence of death there can be no awarenees, no ascendancy of consciousness, no withdrawal from the gridded symbols into the void-without-background."*

—ROYALI's *Religion for Everyone*,
conversations with the Abbod

They called it the Sheleb Incident, Stetson noted, and were happy that the I-A suffered only one casualty. He thought of this as his scout cruiser brought the one casualty back to Marak. A conversation with the casualty kept coming back to him.

"Senior fieldmen last about half as long as the juniors. Very high mortality."

Stetson uttered a convoluted *Prjado* curse.

The medics said there was no hope of saving the field agent *rescued* from Sheleb. The man was alive only by an extremely limited definition. The life and the definition depended entirely upon the womblike

71

crechepod which had taken over most of his vital functions.

Stetson's ship stood starkly in the morning light of Marak Central/Medical Receiving, the casualty still aboard waiting for hospital pickup.

A label on the crechepod identified the disrupted flesh inside as having belonged to an identity called Lewis Orne. His picture in the attached folder showed a blocky, heavy-muscled redhead with off-center features and the hard flesh of a heavy planet native. The flesh in the pod bore little resemblance to the photo, but even in the flaccid repose of demideath, Orne's unguent-smeared body radiated a bizarre aura.

Whenever he moved close to the pod, Stetson sensed power within it and cursed himself for going soft and metaphysical. He had no theory system to explain the feeling, thus dismissed it with a notation in his mind to consult the Psi Branch of the I-A *just in case*. Likely nothing in it . . . but *just in case*. There'd be a Psi officer at the medical center.

A crew from the medical center took delivery on the crechepod and Orne as soon as they got port clearance.

Stetson, moving in his own shock and grief, resented the way the medical crew worked with such casual and cold efficiency. They obviously accepted the *patient* more as a curiosity than anything else. The crew chief, signing the manifest, noted that Orne had lost one eye, all the hair on that side of his head—the left side as noted in the pod manifest—had suffered complete loss of lung function, kidney function, five inches of the right femur, three fingers of the left hand, about one hundred square centimeters of skin on back and thigh, the entire left kneecap and a section of jawbone and teeth on the left side.

The pod instruments showed that Orne had been in terminal shock for a bit over one hundred and ninety *elapsed* hours.

"Why'd you bother with the pod?" a medic asked.

"Because he's alive!"

The medic pointed to an indicator on the pod. "This patient's vital tone is too low to permit operative replacement of damaged organs or the energy drain for regrowth. He'll live for a while because of the pod, but . . ." And the medic shrugged.

"But he *is* alive," Stetson insisted.

"And we can always pray for a miracle," the medic said.

Stetson glared at the man, wondering if that had been a sneering remark, but the medic was staring into the pod through the tiny observation port.

The medic straightened presently, shook his head. "We'll do what we can, of course," he said.

They shifted the pod to a hospital flitter then and skimmed off toward one of the gray monoliths which ringed the field.

Stetson returned to his cruiser's office, an added droop to his shoulders that accentuated his usual slouching stance. His overlarge features were drawn into ridges of sorrow. He slumped into his desk chair, looked out the open port beside him. Some four hundred meters below, the scurrying beetlelike activity of the main port sent up discordant roarings and clatterings. Two rows of other scout cruisers stood in lines just outside the medical receiving area—gleaming red and black needles. Part of the buzzing activity down there would be ground control getting ready to shift his cruiser into that waiting array of ships.

How many of them stopped first in this area to offload casualties? Stetson wondered.

It bothered him that he didn't possess this information. He stared at the other ships without really seeing them, seeing only the dangling flesh, the red gaps in Orne's body as it had been when they'd transferred him from Sheleb's battered soil to the crechepod.

He thought: *It always happens on some routine assignment. We had nothing but a casual suspicion about Sheleb—the fact that only women held high office. A simple, unexplained fact and I lose one of my best agents.*

He sighed, turned to his desk and began composing the report:

"The militant core on the Planet Sheleb has been eliminated. *(Bloody mess, that!)* Occupation force on the ground. *(Orne's right about occupation forces: For every good they do, they create an evil!)* No further danger to Galactic peace expected from this source. *(What can a shattered and demoralized population do?)*

"Reason for Operation: *(bloody stupidity!)* R&R —after two months of contact with Sheleb—failed to detect signs of militancy.

"Major indicators: *(the whole damn spectrum!)*

"1.) A ruling caste restricted to women.

"2.) Disparity between numbers and activities of males and females *far* beyond the Lutig norm!

"3.) The full secrecy/hierarchy/control/security syndrome.

"Senior Field Agent Lewis Orne found that the ruling caste was controlling the sex of offspring at conception (see details attached) and had raised a male slave army to maintain its rule. The R&R agent had been drained of information, replaced with a double and killed. Arms constructed on the basis of that treachery caused critical injuries to Senior Field Agent Orne. He is not expected to survive. I am hereby recommending that Orne receive the Galaxy Medal and that his name be added to the Roll of Honor."

Stetson pushed the report aside. That was enough for ComGo. The commander of galactic operations never went beyond the raw details. The fine print would be for his aides to digest and that could come later. Stetson punched his call box for Orne's service record, set himself to the task he most detested: notifying next of kin. He studied the record, pursing his lips.

"Home Planet: Chargon. Notify in case of accident or death: Mrs. Victoria Orne, mother."

He scanned through the record, reluctant to send the hated message. Orne had enlisted in the Federation Marines at age seventeen standard (a runaway from home) and his mother had given postenlistment consent. Two years later: scholarship transfer to Uni-Galacta, the R&R school here on Marak. Five years of school, one R&R field assignment under his belt, and he had been drafted into the I-A for brilliant detection of militancy on Hamal. Two years later—a crechepod!

Abruptly, Stetson hurled the service record at the gray metal wall across from him; then he got up brought the record back to his desk. There were tears in his eyes. He flipped the proper communications switch, dictated the notification to Central Secretarial, ordered it transmitted Priority One. He went groundside then and got drunk on Hochar brandy, Orne's favorite drink.

The next morning there was a reply from Chargon:

"Lewis Orne's mother too ill to be notified or to travel. Sisters being notified. Please ask Mrs. Ipscott Bullone of Marak, wife of the High Commissioner, to take over for family." It was signed: "Madrena Orne Standish, sister."

With some misgivings, Stetson called the Residency for Ipscott Bullone, leader of the majority party in the Federation Assembly. Mrs. Bullone took the call with blank screen. There was a sound of running water in the background.

Stetson stared into the grayness swimming in his desk screen. He always disliked blank screens. His head ached from the Hochar brandy and his stomach kept insisting this was an idiot call. There *had* to be a mistake.

A baritone husk of a voice came from the speaker beside the screen: "This is Polly Bullone."

Telling his stomach to shut up, Stetson introduced himself, relayed the Chargon message.

"Victoria's boy dying? Here? Oh, the poor thing! And Madrena's back on Chargon—the election. Oh, yes, of course. I'll get right over to the hospital."

Stetson signed off with thanks, broke the contact. He leaned back in his chair, puzzled. *The High Commissioner's wife!* He felt stunned. Something didn't track here. He recalled it then: *The First-Contact! Hamal! A blunderbrain named Andre Bullone!*

Using his scrambler, Stetson called for the follow-up report on Hamal, found that Andre Bullone was a nephew of the High Commissioner. Nepotism began on high, obviously. But there was no apparent influence in Orne's case. A runaway in his teens. Brilliant. Self-motivated. Orne had denied any

76

knowledge of a connection between Andre Bullone and the High Commissioner.

He was telling the truth, Stetson thought. *Orne didn't know about this family connection.*

Stetson continued scanning the report. *A mess!* The nephew had been transferred to a desk job far back in the bureaucracy: report juggler. There was a green check mark beside the transfer notice, indicating *pressure from on high.*

Now—a family linkup between Orne and the Bullones.

Still puzzled, but unable to see a way through the problem, Stetson scrambled an *eyes-only* memo to ComGo, then turned to the *urgent* list atop his work-in-progress file.

As the mythological glossary developed our first primitive understanding of Psi, a transformation occurred. Out of the grimoire came curiosity and the translation of fear into experiment. Men dared explore this terrifying frontier with the analytical tools of the mind. From these largely unsophisticated gropings arose the first pragmatic handbooks out of which we developed Religious Psi.

—HALMYRACH, ABBOD OF AMEL,
Psi and Religion

At the I-A medical center, the oval crechepod containing Orne's flesh dangled from ceiling hooks in a private room. There were humming sounds in the dim, watery green of the room, and rhythmic chuggings, sighings, clackings. Occasionally, a door opened quietly and a white-clad figure would enter, check the graph tapes on the crechepod's instruments, examine the vital connections, then depart.

In the medical euphemism, Orne was *lingering*.

He became a major conversation piece at the interns' rest breaks: "That agent who was hurt on Sheleb, he's still with us. Man, they must build those guys different from the rest of us! . . . Yeah. I heard he only has about one-eighth of his insides—liver, kidneys, stomach, all gone . . . Lay you odds he doesn't last out the month . . . Look at what old sure-thing Tavish wants to bet on!"

On the morning of his eighty-eighth day in the crechepod, the day nurse entered Orne's room for her first routine check. She lifted the inspection hood, looked down at him. The day nurse was a tall, lean-faced professional who had learned to meet miracles and failures with equal lack of expression. She was *just here to observe*. The daily routine with the dying (or already dead) I-A operative had lulled her into a state of psychological unpreparedness for anything but closing out the records.

Any day now, poor guy, she thought.

Orne opened his only remaining eye and she gasped as he said in a low whisper: "Did they clobber those dames on Sheleb?"

"Yes, sir!" the day nurse blurted. "They really did, sir!"

"Another damn mess," Orne said. He closed his eye. His breathing-simulation deepened and heart-demand increased.

The nurse rang frantically for the doctors.

Part of our problem centers on the effort to introduce external control for a system-of-systems that should be maintained by internal balancing forces. We are not attempting to recognize and refrain from inhibiting those self-regulating systems in our species upon which species survival depends. We are ignoring our own feedback functions.

—LEWIS ORNE's *Report on Hamal*

For Orne, there had been an indeterminate period in a blank fog, then a time of pain and the gradual realization that he was in a crechepod. Had to be. He could remember the sudden disrupter explosion on Sheleb . . . the explosion like a silent force thrusting at him—no sound, just an enveloping nothingness.

Good old crechepod. It made him feel safe, shielded from outside perils. Things still went on inside him, though. He could remember . . . *dreams?* He wasn't sure they really were dreams. There was something about a hoe and handles. He tried to recall the elusive thought pattern. He sensed his linkage with the crechepod and, beyond that, a connection with some kind of merciless manipulative system, a *mass effect* reducing all existence to a base level.

Is it possible that Man invented war and was trapped by his own invention? Orne wondered. *Who are we in the I-A to set ourselves up as a board of angels to mediate in the affairs of all sentient life we contact?*

Is it possible we are influenced by our universe in ways we don't readily recognize?

He sensed his brain/mind/awareness churning, visualized all of this activity as a bizarre tool for symbolizing the drives and energy desires of all life. Somewhere within himself, he felt there was an ancient function, a thing of archaic tendencies which remained constant despite the marks of the evolution through which it had passed.

Abruptly, he felt himself in the presence of an overwhelming thought/presence: *The most misguided effort of sentience is the attempt to alter the past, to weed out discrepancies, to insist on fellow-happiness at any price. To refrain from harming others is one thing; to design and order happiness for others and to enforce delivery invites an equal-and-opposite reaction.*

Orne drifted off to sleep with this convoluted thought winding and twisting in his awareness.

The human operates out of complex superiority demands, self-affirming through ritual, insisting upon a rational need to learn, striving for self-imposed goals, manipulating his environment while he denies his own adaptive abilities, never fully satisfied.

—LECTURES OF HALMYRACH,
private publication files of Amel

Orne began to show small but steady signs of recovery. Within a month, the medics ventured an intestinal transplant which increased his response rate. Two months later, they placed him on an *atlotl/gibiril* regimen, forcing the energy transfer which allowed him to regrow his lost fingers and eye, restore his scalp line and erase the other internal-external damage.

Through it all, Orne found himself wrestling with his soul. He felt strangled by the patterns he had once accepted, as though he had passed through profound change which had removed him from the body of his past. All of the assumptions of his former existence took on the character of shadows, passionless and contrary to the new flesh growing within him. He felt that he had been surprised by his own death, and had accepted the total denial of a life which had melted into a sandpile. Now, he was rebuilding, willfully accepting only a one-part definition of existence.

I am one being, he thought. *I exist. That is enough. I give life to myself.*

The thought slipped into him like a fire which bore him forward out of an ancestral cave. The wheel of his life was turning, and he knew it would go full circle.

He felt that he had gone down into the intestines of the universe to see how everything was made.

No more old taboos, he thought. *I have been both alive and dead.*

Fourteen months, eleven days, five hours and two minutes after he had been picked up on Shelab "as good as dead," Orne walked out of the hospital on his own two legs, accompanied by an oddly silent Umbo Stetson.

Under the dark-blue I-A field cape, Orne's coverall uniform fitted his once-muscular frame like a deflated bag. The pixie light had returned to his eyes, though—even to the new eye which had grown parallel with his new awareness. Except for the loss of weight, he appeared to be the old Lewis Orne. It was a close enough resemblance that most former acquaintances could have recognized him after only a moment's hesitation. The internal differences did not show themselves to the casual eye.

Outside the hospital, clouds obscured Marak's greenish sun. It was midmorning. A cold spring wind bent the pile lawn, tugged fitfully at border plantings of exotic flowers around the hospital's landing pad.

Orne paused on the steps above the pad, breathed deeply of the chill air. "Beautiful day," he said. His new kneecap felt strange, a better fit than the old one. He was acutely conscious of all his new parts and the regrowth syndrome which made all crechepod *graduates* share the unjoke label of "twice-born."

Stetson reached out a hand to help Orne down the steps, hesitated, put the hand back in his pocket. Beneath the section chief's look of weary superciliousness there was a note of anxiety. His big features remained set in a frown. The drooping eyelids failed to conceal a sharp, measuring stare.

Orne glanced at the sky to the southwest.

"Flitter ought to be here soon," Stetson said.

A gust of wind tugged at Orne's cape. He staggered, caught his balance. "I *feel* good," he said.

"You look like something left over from a funeral," Stetson growled.

"My funeral," Orne said. He grinned. "Anyway, I was getting tired of that walk-around-style morgue they call a hospital. All of my nurses were married or otherwise paired."

"I'd stake my life that I could trust you," Stetson muttered.

Orne glanced at him, puzzled by the remark. "What?"

"Stake my life," Stetson said.

"No, no, Stet. Stake *my* life. I'm used to it."

Stetson shook his head bearlike from side to side. "Be funny! I trust you, but you deserve a peaceful convalescence."

"Get it off your chest," Orne said. "What's brewing?"

"We've no right to saddle you with an assignment at a time like this," Stetson said.

Orne's voice came out low and amused: "Stet?"

Stetson looked at him. "Huh?"

"Save the noble act for someone who doesn't know you," Orne said. "You've a job for me. All right. You've made the gesture for your conscience."

Stetson managed a wry grin. He said: "The problem is we're desperate and we haven't much time."

"That sounds familiar," Orne said. "But I'm not sure I want to play the old games. What's on your mind?"

84

Stetson shrugged. "Well . . . since you're going to be a houseguest at the Bullones' *any*way, we thought . . . well, we suspect Ipscott Bullone of heading a conspiracy to take over the government, and if you . . ."

"What do you mean *take over the government?*" Orne demanded. "The Galactic High Commissioner *is* the government—subject to the Constitution and the Assemblymen who elected him."

"That's not what I mean."

"What do you mean?"

"Orne, we may have an internal situation which could explode us into another Rim War. We think Bullone's at the heart of it," Stetson said. "We've found eighty-one touchy planets, all old-line steadies that've been in the Galactic League for centuries. And on every damn one of them we've reason to believe there's a gang of traitors who're sworn to overthrow the League. Even on your home planet—Chargon."

"On Chargon?" Orne's whole stance signaled disbelief.

"That's what I said."

Orne shook his head. "What is it you want from me? Do you want me to go home for my convalescence? I haven't been there since I was seventeen, Stet. I'm not sure I . . ."

"No, dammit! We want you as the Bullones' houseguest. And speaking of that, do you mind explaining how they were chosen to ride herd on you?"

"That's odd, you know," Orne said, withdrawing reflexively. "All those trite little jokes in the I-A about old Upshook Ipscott . . . then I discover that his wife went to school with my mother—roommates, for the love of all that's holy!"

"Your mother never mentioned it?"

"It never came up that I can recall."

"Have you met Himself?"

"He brought his wife to the hospital a couple of times. Seems like a nice enough fellow, but somewhat stiff and reserved."

Stetson pursed his lips in thought, glanced to the southwest, back to Orne. He said: "Every school kid knows how the Nathians and the Marakian League fought it out in the Rim Wars—how the old civilization fell apart. It all seems kind of distant now that the Marakian League has become the Galactic League and we're knitting it back together."

"Five centuries is a long time," Orne said, "if you'll pardon a statement of the obvious."

"Maybe it's no farther away than yesterday," Stetson said. He cleared his throat, stared penetratingly at Orne.

Orne wondered why Stetson was moving with such caution. What had he meant by that reference to the Nathians and the Marakians? Something deep troubling him. Why speak of trust?

Stetson sighed, looked away.

Orne said: "You spoke of trusting me. Why? Has this suspected conspiracy involved the I-A?"

"We think so," Stetson said.

"Why?"

"About a year ago, an R&R archæological team was nosing into some ruins on Dabih. The place had been all but vitrified in the Rim Wars, but an entire bank of records from a Nathian outpost escaped." He glanced sidelong at Orne.

"So?" Orne asked when the silence became prolonged.

Stetson nodded as though to himself, said: "The

Rah-Rah boys couldn't make sense out of their discovery. No surprise there. They called in an I-A cryptanalyst. He broke a complicated cipher into which the stuff had been transferred. Then, when the stuff he was reading started making sense, he pushed the panic button without letting on to R&R."

"For something the Nathians wrote five hundred years ago?"

Stetson's drooping eyelids lifted, opening his eyes into a cold, probing stare. He said: "Dabih was a routing station for selected elements of the most powerful Nathian families."

"Routing station?" Orne asked, puzzled.

"For trained refugees," Stetson said. "An old dodge. Been used as long as they've been . . ."

"But five hundred *years*, Stet!"

"I don't care if it was five *thousand* years," Stetson snapped. "We've intercepted message scraps in the past month that were written in the *same* code. The bland confidence of *that!* Wouldn't that gall you?" He shook his head. "And every scrap we've intercepted deals with the coming elections!"

Orne found himself caught up in Stetson's puzzle, excited, interpreting it all through the I-A's prime directive—prevent another Rim War at all costs.

"The upcoming election's crucial," Stetson said.

"But it's only two days off!" Orne protested.

Stetson touched the time-beat repeater at his temple, paused to get the cronosynch, then: "Forty-two hours and fifty minutes to be exact. Some deadline."

"Were there any names in those Dabih records?" Orne asked.

Stetson nodded. "Names of planets, yes. And family

names, but those were translated into a new code system which we haven't broken and may not break. Too simple."

"What do you mean, *too simple?*"

"They're obviously cover names relating to some internal Nathian social understanding. We can translate the Dabih records into words, but how those words have been translated into cover names is beyond us. For example, the code name on Chargon was *Winner.* That ring any bells?"

Orne shook his head from side to side. "No."

"I didn't expect it to," Stetson said.

"What's the code name on Marak?" Orne asked.

"The *Head,*" Stetson said. "Can you make that tie up with Bullone?"

"I see what you mean. Then, how do you . . ."

"They're sure to've changed the names by now anyway," Stetson said.

"Maybe not," Orne said. "They didn't change their cipher system." He shook his head, trying to capture a thought he sensed lurking just beyond his awareness. The thought didn't come to him. He felt drained suddenly by the effort of following Stetson's cautious unveiling of the plot.

"You're right," Stetson murmured. "We'll keep at it, then. Something may show up."

"What leads are you working on?" Orne asked. He knew Stetson was holding back something vital.

"Leads? We've gone back to our history books. They say the Nathians were top-drawer political mechanics. The Dabih records give us a few facts, just enough to tease us into frustration."

"Such as?"

"The Nathians chose cover sites for their trained *refugees* with diabological care. Every one was a planet so torn up by the wars that its inhabitants just wanted to rebuild and forget violence. The instructions to the Nathian families were clear enough, too: dig in, grow up with the adopted culture, develop the political weak spots, build an underground force, train their descendants to take over."

"The Nathians sound long on patience," Orne said.

"By any measurement you use. They set out to bore from within, to make victory out of defeat."

"Refresh me on the history," Orne said.

"The original human stock came from Nathia II. Their mythology calls them Arbs or Ayrbs. Peculiar customs—space wanderers, but with a strong sense of family and loyalty to their own people. Moody types. very volatile, so it says. Go review your seventh grade history. You'll know almost as much as I do."

"On Chargon," Orne said, "our history texts referred to the Nathians as 'one of the factions involved in the Rim Wars.' The impression I got was that they shared the blame just about equally with the Marakian League."

"There are places where that might sound seditious," Stetson said.

"How does it sound to you?" Orne asked.

"The victors always write the history," Stetson said.

"Except perhaps on Chargon," Orne said. "What has you haring after High Commissioner Upshook? And while we're on that question, why're you parceling out your information like a miser giving money to a spendthrift son-in-law?"

Stetson wet his lips with his tongue, said: "One of

Upshook's seven daughters is currently at home. Name of Diana. She's a field leader in the I-A women."

"I seem to've heard of her," Orne said. "I think Mrs. Bullone mentioned the fact she was at home."

"Yes, well . . . one of these Nathian code messages we intercepted had her name as addressee."

"Wheeewww!" Orne exhaled in surprise, then: "Who sent the message? What was the content?"

Stetson coughed. "You know, Lew, we cross-check everything."

"So what else is new?"

"This message was handwritten and signed MOS."

When Stetson didn't go on, Orne said: "And you know who MOS is, that it?"

"Our cross-check gave us an MOS on a routine next-of-kin reply. We followed it down to the original. The handwriting checks out. Name of Madrena Orne Standish."

Orne froze. "Maddie?" He turned slowly to face Stetson. "So *that's* what's eating you."

"We know for certain that you haven't been home since you were seventeen," Stetson said. "We can account for all the significant blocks of time in your life. With us, your record is clean. The question is . . ."

"Permit me," Orne said. "The question is: Will I turn in my own sister if it falls that way?"

Stetson remained silent, staring. And Orne noticed now that the man had retreated behind the mask of I-A senior officer, holding one hand concealed in a uniform pocket. What was in that pocket? A transmitter? A weapon?

"I read you," Orne said. "I remember the oath I took and I know my job: see to it that we don't have another blowup like the Rim Wars. But Maddie in this?"

"No doubt of it," Stetson grated.

Orne thought back to his own childhood. *Maddie?* He remembered a red-headed tomboy, his ready companion for adventure, a fellow conspirator when adults pressed too closely on the secret world of the young.

"Well?" Stetson pressed.

"My family isn't one of these traitor clans you refer to," Orne said. "How can Maddie be mixed up in this?"

"This whole thing is all tangled in politics," Stetson said. "We think it's because of her husband."

"Ahhhh, the Member for Chargon," Orne said. "I've never met him, but I've followed his career with interest . . . and Maddie wrote me and sent a picture when they were married."

"You like this particular sister very much," Stetson said. It was a statement, not a question.

"I have . . . fond memories," Orne said. "She helped me when I ran away."

"Why'd you leave home?" Stetson asked.

Orne sensed the weight behind the question, fought to keep his voice casual. "It was a family thing. I knew what I wanted to do. The family objected."

"You wanted to join the Marines?"

"No, they were just a way into the R&R. I don't like violence. And I don't like women running my life."

Stetson glanced to the southwest where a flitter could be seen approaching. Green sunlight glinted from it. He asked: "Are you willing to . . . infiltrate the Bullone family for . . ."

"Infiltrate!"

"To find out whatever you can about this plot centered on the upcoming election."

"In forty-two hours!"

"Or less."

"Who's my contact?" Orne asked. "I'll be trapped out there at the Residency."

"That mini-transceiver we planted in your neck for the Gienah job," Stetson said. "The medics replaced it at my request while they were putting you back together."

"How nice of them."

"It's functioning," Stetson said. "Anything happens around you, we hear it."

"That'll keep me loyal," Orne said. As he spoke, he experienced the thought that if he just willed the transceiver to leave his flesh, the thing would pop out of his skin like a seed squeezed from ripe fruit. He shook his head. That was a crazy thought!

"That's *not* why it's there," Stetson protested.

Frightened by the waywardness of his own thoughts, Orne touched the hidden stud at his neck, spoke subvocally. He knew a surf-hissing voice was being picked up by an I-A monitor somewhere within beam distance.

"*Hey, eavesdropper! You pay attention while I'm making my play for this Diana Bullone, you hear? You may learn something about the way an expert works.*"

Surprisingly, Stetson answered him: "Don't get so interested in your work that you forget why you're out there."

So Stet was wearing one of these damn devices, too. Didn't the I-A trust anyone anymore?

In terms of human systems, feedback involves complicated unconscious processes, both individual and in a collective or social sense. That individuals can be influenced by such unconscious forces has long been recognized. The large-scale processes and their influence, however, are less well known. We tend to see them only latently in a statistical sense—by population curves, by historial evolution, by changes which stretch across the centuries. We often ascribe such processes to religious forces and have a tendency to avoid examining them analytically.

—Lectures of the ABBOD
(privately circulated)

Mrs. Bullone was a fat little mouse of a woman standing almost in the center of her home's guest room, hands clasped across the paunch of a long dull-silver gown.

Orne thought: *I must remember to call her Polly as she requested.*

She possessed demure gray eyes, grandmotherly gray hair combed straight back in a jeweled net—and that shocking baritone husk of a voice issuing from a tiny mouth. Her figure sloped out from several chins to a matronly bosom, then dropped straight as a bar-

93

rel. The top of her head came just above Orne's dress epaulets.

She said: "We want you to feel perfectly at home with us, Lewis. You're to consider yourself one of the family."

Orne glanced around at the Bullone guest room: low-key furnishings with an old-fashioned selectacol for change of color scheme. A polawindow looked out onto an oval swimming pool. The glass (he was sure it was glass and not a more technologically sophisticated substance) had been muted to dark blue. This imparted a moonlit appearance to the view outside. A contour bed stood against the wall at the right; several built-ins there. A door partly open on the left revealed a wedge of bathroom tiles. Everything about the place seemed traditional and comfortable. He *did* feel at home.

Orne said it: "I already feel at home here. You know, your house is very like our place on Chargon. Just as I remember it. I was really surprised when I saw it from the air as we were coming in. Except for the setting, it's almost identical."

"Your mother and I shared many ideas when we were in school together," Polly said. "We were *very* close friends. Still are."

"You must be to do all this for me," Orne said, his own voice giving him an oddly alienated feeling. Such banality! Such hypocrisy! But the words flowed right on: "I don't know how I'm ever going to repay you for . . ."

"Ah, here we are!" A deep masculine voice boomed from the open door behind Orne. He turned, saw Ipscott Bullone, High Commissioner of the League, suspected conspirator.

Bullone was tall with a face of harsh angles and deep lines. His dark eyes peered from beneath heavy brows and black hair trained in receding waves. He radiated a look of ungainly clumsiness which was probably a political affectation.

He just doesn't strike me as the dictator or conspirator type, Orne thought.

Bullone advanced into the room, his voice filling it. "Glad you made it out all right, son. Hope everything's to your taste. If it isn't, you just say the word."

"It's . . . fine," Orne said.

"Lewis was just telling me how our place is very much like his home on Chargon," Polly said.

"Old-fashioned, but we like it that way," Bullone said. "I don't like the modern trend in architecture. Too mechanical. Give me an old-fashioned tetragon on a central pivot every time."

"You sound just like my family," Orne said.

"Good! Good! We usually keep the main salon turned toward the northeast. View of the capital, you know. But if you want the sun, the shade or a breeze in your room, feel free to turn the house on your own."

"That's very kind of you," Orne said. "We have a sea breeze on Chargon that we usually keep the main salon centered on. We like the air."

"So do we. So do we. You must tell me all about Chargon when we can sit down together, man to man. It'll be good to get your views on things there."

"I'm sure Lewis would like to be left alone for a while now," Polly said. "This is his first day out of the hospital and we mustn't tire him."

She's rushing him out, Orne thought. *She hasn't told him yet that I've been away from home since I was seventeen.*

95

Polly crossed to the polawindow, adjusted it to neutral gray, turned the selectacol until the room's dominant color shifted to green. "There, that's more restful," she said. "If there's anything you need, just ring the bell there by your bed. The autobutle will know what to do or where to find us if it doesn't."

"We'll see you at dinner, then," Bullone said.

They left.

Orne crossed to the window, looked out at the pool. The young woman hadn't returned yet. When the chauffeur-driven limousine flitter had dropped down to the house's landing pad, Orne had seen a parasol and sun hat nodding to each other on the blue tiles beside the pool. The parasol had shielded Polly Bullone. The sun hat had been worn by a shapely young woman in swimming tights. She had rushed off into the house at first sight of the flitter.

Orne thought about the young woman. She had been no taller than Polly, but slender and with golden-red hair caught under the sun hat in a swimmer's chignon. She wasn't beautiful—face too narrow and with suggestions of the father's cragginess. The eyes were overlarge. But her mouth was full-lipped, chin strong. There had been an air of exquisite assurance about her. The total effect had been one of striking elegance—extremely feminine.

So that was his target—Diana Bullone. Where'd she gone in such a hurry?

Orne lifted his gaze to the landscape beyond the pool: wooded hills and, dimly on the horizon, a broken line of mountains. The Bullones lived in costly isolation despite their love of traditional simplicity . . . or perhaps because of it. Urban centers didn't lend themselves to such old-time elegance. But here, centered in kilometers of wilderness and rugged, planned neglect of countryside, they could be what they wanted to be.

They could also be insulated from prying eyes.

Time to report in, Orne thought. He pressed the neck stud for his transceiver, got Stetson, brought him up to date.

"All right," Stetson said. *"Find the daughter. She fits the description of the woman you saw by the pool."*

"I know," Orne said. He broke the connection, wondered at himself. He felt that he had become several people—one of them playing Stetson's game, another off on personal interests, still another observing and disapproving. Through all of this, he felt that some essential core of himself had returned from death to become immersed in life—warm life teeming with beauty and movement. His body performed in one way, but an essential part of him filled with life and force-floated somewhere on a plane which interpreted death as only part of maturing.

It was a sensation of distortion and stretching. He fled from it, changing into light-blue fatigues and letting himself out of the room into a curved yellow hallway. A touch to the time-beat repeater at his temple told him it was shortly before local noon. There was latitude for a bit of scouting before they called lunch. He knew from his brief tour of the house and its similarity to his childhood home that the hallway led into the main living salon. Public rooms and men's quarters would be in this outside ring. Secluded family apartments and women's quarters would occupy the inner circle.

Orne made his way to the salon.

It was a long room built around two sections of the

tetragon. Low divans occupied the space beneath the windows, some facing inward, some outward. Thick pile rugs formed a crazy patchwork of reds and browns throughout the room.

At the far end of the salon, a figure in blue fatigues much like his own stood bent over a metal stand. The figure straightened and a tinkle of music filled the room.

Orne stood entranced at the familiar sound. It transported him in memory back to his childhood. The instrument was a kaithra. His own sisters had played it in a setting such as this one. He recognized the woman at the kaithra—the same red-gold hair, the same figure. It was the young woman he had seen beside the pool. She wielded two mallets in each hand to play the instrument which lay in a long dish of carved black wood on the metal stand, the strings stretched in six banks of five.

Orne, moody and caught in memories, moved up behind her, his footsteps muffled by the thick carpeting. The music possessed a curious rhythm. It suggested figures dancing wildly around firelight, rising, falling, stamping. She struck a final chord, muted the strings.

"That makes me homesick," Orne said.

"Oh!" She whirled, gasped. "You startled me. I thought I was alone."

"Sorry. I was just enjoying the music."

She smiled. "I'm Diana Bullone. You're Lewis Orne."

"Lew to all of your family, I hope," he said. He enjoyed the warmth of her smile.

"Of course . . . Lew." She put the mallets atop the kaithra's strings. "This is a very old instrument. Most people find its music . . well, rather strange. The ability to play it has been handed down for generations in mother's family."

"The kaithra," Orne said. "My sisters play it. Been a long time since I've heard one."

"Of course," she said. "Your mother's . . ." She stopped, appeared confused. "I have to get used to the fact that you're . . . I mean, that we have a strange man around the house who isn't *exactly* strange."

Orne found himself grinning and aware of self-loathing from the inner observer part of his being.

In spite of the severely cut I-A fatigues and hair pulled back into a tight beret-knot, Diana was a handsome woman. She possessed an electric presence. Orne reminded himself that this was Stetson's prime suspect in the Nathian plot. Diana and Maddie? It was too odd a situation to accept casually. He could not afford to like this woman, but he did. She was the daughter of a family which had been kind to him, which was taking him into its own household as an honored guest. And how was such hospitality being repaid? By spying and prying.

He reminded himself that his first loyalty belonged to the I-A and the peace it represented. Another part of him, though. chimed in mockingly—*peace such as that now prevailing on Hamal and Sheleb.*

Rather lamely, he said: "I hope you get over the feeling that I'm a stranger."

"I'm already over it," she said. She stepped forward, linked arms with him, said: "If you feel up to it, I'll give you the deluxe guided tour. This is a really weird house, but I love it."

Music represents an essential part of many Psi experiences which are labeled religion. Through the ecstatic force of rhythmic sounds, we perceive a call directed at powers outside of time and lacking the usual breadth and length compressed into the forms of matter by our corner of the endless dimensions.

—NOAH ARKWRIGHT,
The Forms of I'si

By nightfall, Orne had been reduced to a state of confusion. He found Diana exciting and fascinating, yet the most *comfortable* female companion he had ever met. She liked swimming, the bloodless hunting of *paloika*, the taste of *ditar* apples. She betrayed a disdainful attitude toward the older generation and I-A officialdom which she said she'd never before revealed to anyone.

They had laughed like fools over utter nonsense.

Orne returned to his room to change for dinner, stopped at the polawindow, which he tuned to clear transmission. The quick darkness of these latitudes had pulled an ebony blanket over the landscape. Distant cityglow painted a short yellow horizon off to the left. An orange halo remained on the peaks where Marak's three moons would rise.

Am I falling in love with this woman? Orne asked himself.

Again, he sensed the fragmentation of his being—and this time felt the pull of his childhood training added to all of the other forces at war within him. The ritual training of Chargon came back to him with all of its mystery.

He thought: *I am that. I am the consciousness of self which senses the Absolute and knows the Supreme Wisdom. I am the all-one impersonal I which is God.*

It came straight out of the ancient rites which transferred kingly powers into religious terms, but he felt that the old concepts had taken on new meanings.

"I am God," he whispered and he sensed forces writhing within him. Even as he spoke, he realized the words made no reference to his ego-identity-self. The *I* of this awareness was outside usual human concerns.

Without understanding its significance, Orne realized he had experienced a *religious event*. He knew the Psi definitions taught in the I-A, but this experience shook him.

He wanted to call Stetson, not to report but to talk out his own confusions about his role in this household. This thought made him acutely aware that Stetson or an aide had eavesdropped on his afternoon with Diana.

The autobutle called dinner, distracting Orne from a sensation that he had fallen from grace. He changed hurriedly into a fresh lounge uniform, found his way to the small salon across the house. The Bullones already were seated around an old-fashioned bubbleslot table set with real candles (they smelled of incense) and golden *shardi* service. Two of Marak's three moons could be seen out the window climbing swiftly over the peaks.

"Welcome to you and may you find health in our

house," Bullone said, rising until Orne had seated himself.

"You've turned the house," Orne said.

"We like the moonrise," Polly said. "It's romantic, don't you think?" She glanced at Diana.

Diana looked down at her plate. She wore a low-cut gown of *firemesh* that set off her red hair. A single strand of *Reinach* pearls gleamed at her throat.

Orne, who had taken the seat opposite her, thought: *Lord, what a handsome woman she is.*

Polly, on Orne's right, appeared younger and softer in a green stola gown that hazed her barrel contours. Bullone, on the left, wore black lounging shorts and knee-length *kubi* jacket of golden pearl cloth. Everything about the people and the setting reeked of wealth and power.

For a moment, Orne saw a confirmation of Stetson's suspicions. Bullone might go to any length to maintain this luxury.

Orne's entrance had interrupted an argument between Polly and her husband. As soon as Orne was comfortably seated, they went right on with the argument. Rather than embarrassing him, this lack of inhibition made Orne feel more at home, more accepted.

Diana caught Orne's eye, glanced left and right at her parents, grinned.

"But I'm not running for office this time," Bullone was saying, his voice heavy with strained patience. "Why do we have to clutter up the evening with all of those people just to . . ."

"Our election night parties are traditional," Polly said.

"I'd just like to relax quietly at home for once,"

Bullone said. "I'd like to take it easy with my family and not have to . . ."

"It's not as though it was a *big* party," Polly said. "I've kept the list down to fifty."

Bullone groaned.

Diana said: "Daddy, this is an important election. How could you *possibly* relax? There're seventy-three seats at issue, the whole balance. If things go wrong in just the Aikes sector . . . why . . . you could be sent back to the floor. You'd lose your job as . . . I mean someone else would take over and . . ."

"Welcome to the damn job," Bullone said. "It's one giant headache." He smiled at Orne. "Sorry to burden you with this perennial squabble, m'boy, but the women of this family run me ragged if I let them. From what I hear, you've had a pretty busy day, too. Hope we're not tiring you." He smiled paternally at Diana. "Your first day out of the hospital and all."

"Diana sets quite a pace, but I've enjoyed it," Orne said.

"We're taking the small flitter on a tour of the wilderness area tomorrow," Diana said. "I'll do the driving and Lew can relax."

"Be sure you're back in plenty of time for the party," Polly said.

Bullone turned to Orne. "You see?"

"Now, Scottie," Polly said, "you can't have . . ." She broke off at the sound of a low bell from an alcove behind her. "That'll be for me. Excuse me, please. No, don't get up."

Diana bent toward Orne, said; "If you want, we can have a special meal prepared for you. I asked the hospital and they said you were under no dietary restrictions." She nodded toward Orne's untouched dinner which had emerged from the bubbleslot beside his table setting.

"Oh, this is quite all right," Orne said. He could not hear Polly in the alcove. She had a security cone for certain. He bent to his dinner: meat in an exotic sauce which he couldn't place, *Sirik* champagne, *ataloka au semil* . . . luxury piled upon luxury.

Presently, Polly resumed her seat.

"Anything important?" Bullone asked.

"Only a cancellation for tomorrow night. Professor Wingard is ill."

"I'd just as soon they canceled it down to the four of us," Bullone said. "I want some time to chat with Lewis."

Unless this is a clever pose, that doesn't sound like a man who wants to grab more power. Orne thought.

For the first time, Orne began wondering if Stetson had lied, if this were part of some elaborate political in-fighting process with Stetson and friends at the heart of it. What if a cabal in the I-A were plotting a coup? *No!* He knew he had to stop looking for phantoms and proceed just by what he learned—datum by datum.

Polly glanced at her husband, said: "Scottie, you should take more pride in your office, I swear it. You're an important man and it helps at times to reflect this."

"If it weren't for you, my dear, I'd be a nobody and prefer it," Bullone said, smiling fondly at his wife.

"Oh, now, Scottie," she said.

Bullone grinned at Orne, said: "Compared to my wife, Lewis, I'm a political idiot. Never saw anyone who could call the turn the way she does. It runs in her family. Her mother was the same way and her

104

grandmother! Now, there was a true genius in politics."

Orne stared at him, fork raised from the plate and motionless. A sudden idea had exploded in his mind. *It couldn't be!* he thought. *It just couldn't be!*

"You must know something of this political life, Lew," Diana said. "Wasn't your father once Member for Chargon?"

"Yes," Orne murmured. "He died in office."

"I'm sorry," she said. "I didn't mean to open old wounds."

"It's quite all right," Orne said. He shook his head from side to side, still caught in the throes of his explosive idea. *It couldn't be, but . . . the pattern was almost identical.*

"Do you feel all right, Lewis?" Polly asked. "You're suddenly so pale."

"Just tired," Orne said. "Guess I'm not used to so much activity."

Diana put her fork down, a stricken look on her face. "Oh, Lew! And I've been a beast keeping you so busy today, your first day out of the hospital."

Bullone said: "Don't stand on ceremony in this house, Lewis."

Polly looked concerned, said: "You've been very sick and we understand. If you're tired, Lewis, you go right on to bed. Perhaps we could bring you a little hot broth, later."

Orne glanced around the table, met anxious attention in each face. They were really concerned about him and no mistaking it. He felt torn between duty and the simple demands of humanity. In their own context, these were warm and honest people, but if they . . . Confused, Orne pushed his chair back, said: "Mrs.

Bullone . . ." then remembered she'd asked him to call her Polly. "Polly, if you really don't mind . . ."

"Mind!" she barked "You scoot along."

"May we get you anything?" Bullone asked.

"No. no, really." Orne stood, feeling rubbery in his knees and very aware of the *better* fit in his regrown kneecap.

"I'll see you in the morning, Lew," Diana said. She managed to convey both the concern of a hostess in these words and something warmly personal, a private message. Orne wasn't sure he wanted that private message.

"In the morning," he agreed.

He turned away, thinking: *Lord, what a desirable woman!*

As he started down the hall, he heard Bullone say in a heavily paternal voice: "Di, perhaps you'd better not take that boy all over the place tomorrow. After all, he *is* here for a convalescent rest."

Her answer was lost as Orne entered the hall, closed the door.

In the privacy of his room, Orne pressed the transceiver stud at his neck, said: *"Stet?"*

A voice hissed in his ears on the surf-beat carrier wave: *"This is Mr. Stetson's relief. Orne, isn't it?"*

"Yes, this is Orne. I want a recheck right away on those Nathian records the archaeologists recovered from Dabih. Find out if Sheleb was one of the planets they seeded."

"Right. Hang on."

There was a long silence, then: *"Lew, this is Stet. How come that question about Sheleb?"*

"Was it on the Nathian list?"

"Negative. Why'd you ask?"

106

"Are you sure? It'd explain a lot of things."

"Sheleb is not on their lists . . . but, wait a minute."
Silence, then: *"Sheleb is on the course-line cone to Auriga and Auriga was on their list. We've reason to doubt they put anyone down on Auriga. But if their ship ran into trouble . . ."*

"That's it!" Orne snapped.

"Stop using open voice!" Stetson ordered. *"Sub-vocal only. They can't tap this system, but they know it exists. We can't have them get suspicious because you talk to yourself."*

"Sorry," Orne said. "I just knew Sheleb had to be . . ."

"Why? What've you discovered?"

"I've had an idea that frightens me," Orne said. "Remember that the women who ruled Sheleb were breeding male or female offspring by controlling the sex at conception. In fact, it was that imbalance which . . ."

"You don't have to remind me of something we'd rather have buried and forgotten," Stetson interrupted. *"Why is that so important right now?"*

"Stet, what if your Nathian underground is composed entirely of women bred in that same way? And what if their own men don't even know about it? What if Sheleb were just a place which got out of hand because the women there had lost contact with their main element? They were an R&R discovery."

"Holy Mother Marak," Stetson said. *"Do you have evidence to sub . . ."*

"Nothing but a hunch," Orne said. "Can you get a list of the guests invited to the Bullones' election party tomorrow?"

"Yes, we can get it. Why?"

"Examine it for women who masterminded their husbands in politics. Let me know how many and who."

"Lew, that's not enough to . . ."

"It's all we have to go on at this point," Orne said He paused as a new thought struck him. *"There may be one other thing. Don't forget that the Nathians came from nomad ancestry. The traces will still be there."*

We have a very ancient saying: The more God, the more devil; the more flesh, the more worms, the more property, the more anxiety; the more control, the more that needs control.

—THE ABBODS OF AMEL,
Psi Commentary

Day began early for the Bullones.

In spite of its being election day, the High Commissioner took off for his office an hour after dawn, passing a sleepy-eyed Orne in the main hallway with a bright "Good morning, son. Did you sleep well?"

Orne admitted that he had slept well. He could see Diana and Polly standing in the main salon doorway.

"I have to be going," Bullone said. "See what I mean about this damn job owning you?"

Diana came down the hall followed by Polly, both with questions about Orne's health. They all went outdoors to see Bullone into his limousine flitter. The sky was cloudless and there was a smell of green plants in the air with a faint flower perfume.

"We're going to take it easy today, Lew," Diana said. "I've had my orders."

She took his hand as they went up the steps after her father's departure. Orne found himself enjoying her hand in his—enjoying the tactile contact far too much for his peace of mind. He withdrew his hand at the door, stood aside, said: "Lead on."

"First, breakfast," she said. "We have to get your strength back."

I have to watch myself, Orne thought. *This whole family is too open and charming.*

He thought suddenly of the charming women on Sheleb—before they had turned on him. His body remembered pain.

"I think a picnic is just what your doctor ordered today," Diana said. "There's a little lake with grassy banks out there. We'll take viewers and a couple of good novels, or anything else you might want to read. This'll be a lazy, do-nothing day."

Orne hesitated. "What about your big party?"

"Mother has that well in hand."

Orne glanced around. Polly had gone inside with a last "Hurry along, you two. Breakfast for you in just a few minutes."

Orne thought of the things that might occur today in this house, things he should observe. But, no . . . if he had analyzed the situation correctly, Diana represented a weak link. Time was closing in on him, too. By tomorrow, the Nathians could have the government under their complete control.

He knew he had to make an immediate choice. He said: "Friendly native guide, my life is in your hands."

And he thought: *I hope I'm not a prophet.*

Orne found it warm beside the lake. Purple and orange flowers patterned the grassy bank above him. The water reflected a far shore of dark bushes. Small creatures flitted and cheeped in the brush and trees. There was a *groomis* in the reeds at the lower end of the lake. Every now and then it honked like an old man clearing his throat.

Diana lay on the ground mat they'd spread for their picnic. Her hands were clasped behind her head, eyes closed. The red-gold hair lay in a spray around her face.

"When we were all girls at home we used to picnic

here almost every Eightday," Diana said. "Weather permitting, of course. They make it rain here too much for my liking sometimes."

Orne sat down beside her, faced the lake. He felt deeply uneasy. The pattern was *so* clear. *Like Sheleb, like home, like here,* he thought.

"We girls made a raft over on the other side of the lake," Diana said. She sat up, stared across the water. "You know, I think pieces of it are still there. See?" She pointed to a jumble of logs. As she gestured, her hand brushed Orne's.

Something like an electric shock passed between them.

Without knowing exactly how it happened, Orne found his arms around Diana, their lips pressed together in a lingering kiss. Panic came close to the surface in Orne. He broke away.

"I didn't plan for that to happen," Diana whispered.

"Nor I," Orne muttered. He shook his head. "Lord! Sometimes things get in an awful mess!"

Diana blinked. "Lew . . . don't you . . . like me?"

He ignored the monitoring transceiver, spoke his mind. *They'll just think it's part of the act,* he thought. The thought was bitter.

"Like you?" he said. "I'm in love with you."

She sighed, leaned against his shoulder. "Then what's wrong? You're not already married. Mother had your service record checked." Diana smiled impishly, leaning back to look up at him. "Mother has second sight."

Bitterness remained like a sour taste in Orne's mouth. He could see the pattern so clearly. He said; "Di, I ran away from home when I was seventeen."

"I know, darling. Mother's told me all about you."

111

"You don't understand," he said, "My father died just before I was born. He was . . ."

"It must've been very hard on your mother," she said. "All alone with her family . . . and a new baby on the way."

"They'd known for a long time," Orne said. "My father had *Broach's* disease. They found out about it too late. It was already into the central nervous system."

"How horrible," Diana whispered. "So they planned for you, of course—to have a son, I mean."

Orne's mind felt suddenly like a fish out of water. He found himself grasping at a thought that flopped around just out of reach, then was his own, but still struggling. "Dad was Member for Chargon," he whispered. He felt as though he were living a dream. His voice remained low, shocked. "From when I first began to talk, Mother started grooming me to take his place in public life."

"And you objected to all of that arranging and managing," Diana said.

"I hated it! First chance, I ran away. One of my sisters married a fellow who's now Member for Chargon. And I hope he enjoys it!"

"That'll be Maddie," Diana said.

Orne remembered what Stetson had said about a ciphered note between Diana and Maddie. The thought chilled him.

"How well do you know Maddie?" Orne asked.

"I know her *very* well. Lew, what's wrong with you?"

"Politics," he said. "You'd expect me to play the same game, you calling the shots. Shoot for the top, cut and scramble, claw and dig."

"By this time tomorrow all of that may not be necessary," she said.

Orne sensed the sudden hiss of the carrier wave in his neck transceiver, but there was no accompanying voice from whoever was monitoring.

"What's happening . . . tomorrow?" he asked.

"The election, silly. Lew, you're acting very strange. Are you sure you're feeling well?" She put a hand to his forehead. "Perhaps we'd best . . ."

"Just a minute," Orne said, taking her hand from his forehead and holding it. "About us . . ."

She squeezed his hand.

Orne swallowed.

Diana withdrew her hand, touched his cheek. "I think my parents already suspect. We're notorious love-at-first-sighters in this family." She studied him fondly. "You don't feel feverish, but maybe we'd better . . ."

"What a dope I am," Orne muttered, "I just realized *I* must be a Nathian!"

She stared at him. "You *just* realized?"

He said: "I *knew* it . . . I knew it and didn't want to know it. When you realize a thing . . . that's when you have to accept it."

"Lew, I don't understand you," she said.

There was a hissing gasp in Orne's transceiver, quickly cut off.

"The identical patterns in our families," he said. "Even to the houses, for the love of heaven! There's the real key. What a dope I've been!" He snapped his fingers. "*The head!* Polly! Your mother's the grand boss woman of the whole thing!"

"But, darling . . . of course. She . . . I thought you . . ."

113

"You'd better get me back to her and fast," Orne said. He touched the stud at his neck, but Stetson's voice intruded.

"Great work, Lew! We're moving in a special shock force. Can't take any chances with . . ."

Orne spoke aloud in panic: "Stet! No troops! You get out to the Bullones', and you get there alone."

Diana jumped to her feet, backed away from him.

"What do you mean?" Stetson demanded.

"I'm saving our stupid necks," Orne barked. "Alone! You hear me? Or we'll have a worse mess than any Rim War!"

Diana said: "Lew, who're you talking to?"

He ignored her, demanded: "You hear me, Stet?"

"Does that girl know you're talking to me?" Stetson asked.

"Of course she knows I'm talking to you! Now, you come out here alone and no troops!"

"All right, Lew. I don't know what the situation is, but I still trust you even though you've admitted . . . well, you knew I was listening. The O-force is going on standby. I'll be at the Bullone residence in ten minutes, but I won't be alone. ComGo will be with me." Pause. *"And he says you'd better know what you're doing."*

*There is a devil in anything we don't understand.
The background of the universe appears black to
the lidded eye. Thus, we perceive a Satanic
backdrop from which all insecurity originates. It is
from this area of constant menace that we achieve
our vision of hell. To defeat this devil, we strive for
the illusion of all-knowing. In the face of an infinite
universe imminent beyond the Satonic backdrop,
the never-ending All must remain illusion—only
illusion and no more. Accept this and the backdrop
falls.*

—THE ABBOD HALMYRACH,
Religion into Psi

It was an angry group in a corner of the Bullone
main salon. Louvered shades and muted polawindows
reduced the green glare of the noon sun. In the
background there was the hum of air conditioning and
the gentle mechanical sounds of roboservants preparing for the night's election party.

Stetson leaned against the wall beside a divan,
hands jammed deeply into the pockets of his wrinkled
and patched fatigues. The wagon tracks furrowed his
high forehead. Near Stetson, Admiral Sobat Spencer,
the I-A's Commander of Galactic Operations, paced
the floor. ComGo was a bull-necked bald man with
wide blue eyes, a deceptively mild voice. His pacing
over the patchwork carpeting carried the intensity of a
caged animal—three steps out, three steps back.

Polly Bullone sat on the divan, her mouth pulled into a straight line of angry disapproval. She held her
hands clasped so tightly in her lap that the knuckles
115

showed white. Diana stood beside her mother, fists clenched at her sides. She quivered with fury. Her gaze remained fixed, glaring at Orne.

"So *my* stupidity set up this little conference," Orne said. He stood about five paces from Polly, hands on hips. The Admiral pacing away at his right was beginning to wear on his nerves. "But you'd all better hear me out." He glanced at ComGo. "*All* of you."

Admiral Spencer stopped pacing, glowered at Orne. "I have yet to hear a good reason for not tearing this place apart and getting to the bottom of this situation."

"You . . . you traitor, Lewis," Polly husked.

"I'm inclined to agree with you, Madame," Spencer said. "Only from a different viewpoint." He glanced at Stetson. "Any word yet on Scottie Bullone?"

"They'll call me the minute they find him," Stetson said. He sounded cautious, brooding.

"You were invited to the party here tonight, weren't you, Admiral?" Orne asked.

"What's that have to do with anything?" Spencer demanded.

"Are you prepared to imprison your wife and daughters for conspiracy?" Orne asked.

A tight smile played around Polly's lips.

Spencer opened his mouth, closed it without speaking.

"The Nathians are mostly women," Orne said. "Your womenfolk are among them."

The Admiral looked like a man who'd been kicked in the stomach. "What . . . evidence?" he whispered.

"I have the evidence," Orne said. "I'll come to it in a moment."

116

"Nonsense," the Admiral blustered. "You can't possibly carry out . . ."

"You'd better listen to him, Admiral," Stetson said. "One thing you have to say about Orne, he's worth listening to."

"Then he'd better make sense!" Spencer growled.

"Here's the way it goes," Orne said. "The Nathians are mostly women. There were only a few accidental males and a few planned ones like me. That's why there were no family names to trace—just a tight little female society, all working to positions of power through their men."

Spencer cleared his throat, swallowed. He appeared powerless to take his attention from Orne's mouth.

"My analysis," Orne said, "says that about thirty or forty years ago the conspirators first began breeding a few males, grooming them for really choice top positions. Other Nathian males—the accidents where sex-determination failed—didn't learn about the conspiracy. The new ones, however, became full-fledged members when they reached maturity. That's the course they had planned for me, I believe."

Polly glared at him, looked back at her hands.

Diana looked away when Orne tried to catch her eye.

Orne said: "That part of their plan was scheduled to come to a head with this election. If they pulled this one off, they could move in more boldly."

"You're in this way over your head, boy," Polly growled. "You're too late to do anything about us. Anything!"

"We'll see about that!" Spencer snapped. He seemed to have regained his self-control. "Some key

117

arrests, the full glare of publicity on your . . ."

"No," Orne said. "You're not thinking clearly, Admiral. She's right. It's too late for that approach. It probably was too late a hundred years ago. These women were too firmly entrenched even then."

Spencer stiffened, glared at Orne. "Young man, if I give the word, this place will be a shambles."

"I know," Orne said. "Another Hamal, another Sheleb."

'We can't just ignore this!" Spencer snarled.

"Perhaps not ignore it," Orne said. "But we'll do something close to that. We have no choice. It's time we learned about the hoe and the handle."

"The *what?*" Spencer blared.

"It's right there in the I-A curriculum," Orne said. "Primitive societies discovered this way out of the constant temptation toward lethal violence. One village would make the head of the hoe, the next village down the line would make only the handles. Neither would think of invading the other's special area of manufacture."

Polly looked up, studied Orne's face. Diana appeared confused.

"You know what I think?" Spencer asked. "In your attempt to confuse this issue you've just proved that once a Nathian, you're always a Nathian."

"There's no such thing," Orne said. "Five hundred years of crossbreeding with other peoples saw to that. Now, there's merely a secret society of extremely astute political scientists." He smiled wryly at Polly, glanced back to Spencer. "Think of your own wife, sir. In all honesty, would you be ComGo today if she hadn't guided your career?"

Spencer's face darkened. He drew in his chin, tried

118

to stare Orne down, failed. Presently, he chuckled wryly.

"Sobie is beginning to come to his senses as I knew he would," Polly said. "You're just about through, Lewis. We'll deal with the ones we have to deal with, and you're not one of them."

"Don't underestimate your future son-in-law," Orne said.

"Ha!" Diana barked. "I *hate* you, Lewis Orne!"

"You'll get over that," Orne said, his voice mild.

"Ohhhhhh!" Diana quivered with fury.

"I think I hold most of the trump," Spencer said, his attention on Polly.

"You hold very little if you don't understand the situation fully," Orne said.

Spencer turned a speculative stare on Orne. "Explain."

"Government's a dubious glory," Orne said. "You pay for your power and wealth by balancing on the sharp edge of the blade. That great amorphous thing out there—the people—has turned and swallowed many governments. They can do it in the flash of an angry uprising. The way you prevent that is by giving *good* government, not perfect government—but *good*. Otherwise, sooner or later, your turn comes. It's a point that political genius, my mother, made frequently. It stuck with me." He frowned. "My objection to politics was the compromises you make to get elected . . . and I never liked women running my life."

Stetson moved out from the wall. It's pretty clear," he said. Heads turned toward him. "To stay in power, the Nathians had to give us fairly good government. Admit it. The fact is obvious. On the other hand, if we expose them, we give a bunch of political amateurs, every fanatic and power-hungry demagogue in the universe, just the weapons they need to sweep them into office."

"After that, chaos," Orne said. "So we let the Nathians continue—with two minor alterations."

"We alter nothing," Polly said.

"You haven't learned the lesson of the hoe and the handle," Orne said.

"And you haven't learned the lesson of real political power," Polly countered. "It occurs to me, Lewis, that you don't have a leg to stand on. You have me, but you'll get nothing out of me. The rest of the organization can go on without me. You don't dare expose us. You'd discredit too many important people. We hold the whip hand."

"We have the hoe *and* the handle," Orne said. "The I-A could have ninety percent of your organization in *protective* custody within ten days."

"You couldn't find them!" Polly snapped.

"How, Lew?" Stetson asked.

"Nomads," Orne said. "This house is a glorified tent. Men on the outside, women on the inside. Look for inner courtyard construction. It may be instinctive with Nathian blood."

"Is that enough?" Spencer asked.

"Add an inclination for odd musical instruments," Orne said. "The kaithra, the tambour, the oboe—all nomad instruments. Add female dominance of the family, an odd twist on the nomad heritage, but not unique. Dig into political backgrounds where women have guided their men to power. We'll miss damn few of them."

Polly stared at him with open mouth.

Spencer said: "Things are moving too fast for me. I know just one thing for sure. I'm dedicated to preventing another Rim War. That's my oath. If I have to jail every last one of . . ."

"An hour after this conspiracy became known, you wouldn't be in a position to jail anyone," Orne said. "The husband of a Nathian! You'd be in jail yourself or more likely dead at the hands of a mob."

Spencer paled.

Stetson nodded his agreement with Orne.

"Tell us about the hoe and the handle," Polly said. "What's your suggestion for compromise?"

"Number one: veto power on any candidate you put up," Orne said. "Number two: You can never hold more than half of the top offices."

"Who vetoes our candidates?" Polly asked.

"Admiral Spencer, Stet, myself . . . anyone else we deem trustworthy," Orne said.

"You think you're God or something?" Polly demanded.

"No more than you do," Orne said. "I remember my mother's lessons well. This is a check and balance system. You cut the pie, we get first choice on which pieces to take. One group makes the head of the hoe, another makes the handle. We assemble it together."

There was a protracted silence broken when Spencer said: "It doesn't seem right just to . . ."

"No political compromise is ever totally right," Orne said.

"You keep patching things that always have flaws in them," Polly said. "That's how government is." She chuckled, glanced at Orne. "All right, Lewis, we accept." She looked at Spencer, who shrugged glumly.

121

Polly returned her attention to Orne, said: "Just answer me one question, Lewis: How'd you know I was boss lady?"

"Easy," Orne said. "Those records we found said the . . . Nathian"—he'd almost said *traitor*—"family on Marak carried the code name 'The Head.' Your name, Polly, contains the ancient word *Poll* which means 'head.' "

Polly shot a demanding look at Stetson. "Is he always that sharp?"

"Every time," Stetson said.

"If you want to go into politics, Lewis," Polly said, "I'd be delighted to . . ."

"I'm already in politics," Orne growled. "What I want now is to settle down with Di and catch up on some of the living I've missed."

Diana stiffened, addressed the wall beyond Orne: "I never want to see, hear *from* or hear *of* Lewis Orne ever again! That is final, emphatically final!"

Orne's shoulders drooped. He turned away, stumbled and abruptly collapsed full length on the thick carpets. A collective gasp came from behind him.

Stetson shouted: "Call a doctor! They warned me at the hospital that he was still very weak."

There was the sound of Polly's heavy footsteps running toward the communications alcove in the hall.

"Lew!" It was Diana's voice. She dropped to her knees beside him, soft hands fumbling at his neck, his head.

"Turn him over and loosen his collar," Spencer said. "Give him air."

Gently, they turned Orne onto his back. He looked pale.

Diana loosened his collar, buried her face in his neck. "Oh, Lew, I'm sorry," she sobbed. "I didn't mean it. Please, Lew . . . please don't die. Please!"

Orne opened his eyes, looked up through the red-gold haze of Diana's hair at Spencer and Stetson. There was the sound of Polly's voice giving rapid instructions at the communications center. Orne felt Diana's cheek warm against his neck, the dampness of her tears. Slowly, deliberately, Orne winked at the two men.

Diana shook convulsively against his neck. Her movement activated the transceiver stud. Orne heard the carrier wave hiss in his ears. The sound filled him with anger and he thought: *That damn thing has to go! I wish it were at the bottom of the deepest sea on Marak!*

As he thought this, Orne felt an abrupt vacuum in his flesh where the transceiver had been. The hissing carrier wave cut off sharply. With an abrupt feeling of blank shock, Orne realized the tiny instrument was gone.

A slow sensation of awareness flooded through him. He thought: *Psi! For the love of all that's holy, I'm a Psi!*

Gently, he disengaged himself from Diana, allowed her to help him to a sitting position.

"Oh, Lew," she whispered, stroking his cheek.

Polly appeared behind them. "Doctor's on his way. He said to keep the patient warm and inactive. Why's he sitting up?"

Orne only half-heard them. He thought: *I'll have to go to Amel. No helping that.* He didn't know how he was going to do it, but he knew it would happen.

To Amel.

123

Death has many aspects: Nirvana, the endless wheel of Life, the balance between organism and thinking as a pure activity, tension/relaxation, pain and pleasure, goal-seeking and abnegation. The list is inexhaustible.

—NOAH ARKWRIGHT,
Aspects of Religion

The instant he stepped out of the transport's shields into the warmth of Amel's sunlight on the exit ramp, Orne felt the Psi forces at play in this place. It was like being caught in competing magnetic fields. He caught the ramp's handrail as dizziness held him. The sensation passed and he stared down some two hundred meters at the glassy tricrete of the spaceport. Heat waves shimmered off the glistening surface, baking the air even at his height. No wind stirred the air, but hidden gusts of psi force howled against his recently awakened senses.

When he had broached the subject of Amel, his affairs had moved abruptly and with a mysterious fluidity in that direction. Psi detection and amplification equipment had been brought to him and concealed within his flesh. No one had remarked on the disappearance of the transceiver from his neck and he had not asked to have it replaced.

A technician from the Psi Branch of I-A had been found to train Orne in the use of the new equipment, how to select out the first sharp signals of primary psi detection, how to focus on discrete elements of this new spectrum.

Orders had been cut, signed by Stetson and Spencer—even by Scottie Bullone—although Orne been made aware that such orders were a *mere formality*.

It had been a busy time—meeting his new responsibilities of political selection, preparing for his wedding to Diana, learning the inner workings of the I-A which he had known before only through their surface currents, coming to grips with a new and peculiar kind of fear which arose from his psi awareness.

As he stood on the landing ramp above Amel's spaceport, Orne recalled that fear clearly. He shuddered. Amel crawled with skin-creeping sensations. Weird urges flickered through his mind like flashes of heat lightning One second, he wanted to grunt like a wallowing *kiriffa*; the next instant he felt laughter welling in him while simultaneously a sob tore at his throat.

He thought: *They warned me it would be bad at first*.

Psi training did not ease the fear; it only made him more aware. Without the training, his mind might have confused the discrete sensations, combined them into a blend of awe-fear—perfectly logical emotions for an acolyte disembarking on the *priest planet*.

All around him now was holy ground, sanctuary for all the religions of the known universe (and, some said, for all of the religions in the unknown universe).

Orne forced his attention onto the inner focus as he had been taught to do. Slowly, the crushing awareness dimmed to background annoyance. He drew in a deep breath of the hot, dry air. It was vaguely unsatisfying as though lacking an essential element to which his lungs were accustomed.

Still holding tightly to the rail, he waited to make certain the ghost urges had been subdued. Who knew what one of those compelling sensations might thrust upon him? The glistening inner surface of the opened port beside him reflected his image, distorting it slightly in a way that accepted his differences from the slender norm. The reflected image gave him the appearance of a demigod reincarnated from Amel's ancient past: square and solid with corded neck muscles. A faint scar marked the brow line of his closely cropped red hair. Other tiny scars on his bulldog face were visible because he knew where to look. His memory told him of more scars on his heavy body, but he felt completely recovered from Sheleb—although he knew Sheleb had not recovered from him. There was a humorous observation in the I-A that senior field agents could be detected by the number of scars and medical patches they carried. No one had ever made a similar observation about the numerous worlds where the I-A had interceded.

He wondered if Amel could require that *treatment*, or if the I-A could intercede here. Neither question had a certain answer.

Orne studied the scene around him, still waiting out the psi control. The transport's ramp commanded a sweeping view—a scratchwork of towers, belfries, steeples, monoliths, domes, ziggurats, pagodas, stupas, minarets, dagobas . . . They cluttered a flat plain that stretched to a horizon dancing in the heat waves. Golden sunlight danced off bright primary colors and weathered pastels: buildings in tile and stone, tricrete and plasteel and the synthetics of a thousand thousand civilizations.

The yellow sun, Dubhe, stood at the meridian in a cloudless blue sky. It hammered through Orne's toga with oppressive warmth. The toga was a pale aqua and he resented the fact that he could wear no other garment here. The color marked him as a *student* and he did not feel that he was here to study in the classic sense. But that had been a requirement of admission to Amel. The weight of the garment held perspiration to his body.

One step away along the ramp the escalfield hummed softly, ready to drop him into the bustle at the foot of the transport. Priests and passengers were engaged in a ceremony down there—initiation of new students. Orne didn't know if he would have to undergo such a rite. The portmaster's agent had told him to take his own time in disembarking.

What were they doing down there?

He could hear a throbbing drumchant and a singsong keening almost hidden under the machinery clatter of the port.

As he listened, Orne experienced an abrupt sensation of dread at the unknown which awaited him in the narrow, twisted streets and jumbled buildings of the religious warren. Stories that leaked out of Amel carried such hints of forbidden mystery and power that Orne knew his emotions were tainted. This dread, however, he knew well. It had begun on Marak.

He had been seated in ordinary surroundings at his desk in his bachelor officer quarters. His eyes had been directed without focus at the parklike landscape outside his window—the I-A university grounds. Marak's green sun, low in the afternoon quadrant, had seemed distant and cold. Amel had seemed just as distant—a place to go after his wedding and honeymoon. He had a permanent assignment to the I-A's antiwar college as a lecturer on "Exotic Clues to War."

Abruptly, he had turned away from his desk to frown at the stiffly regulation room. Something in it had gone awry and he couldn't focus on quite what it was. Everything seemed so much in the expected pattern: the gray walls, the sharp angles of the bunk, the white bedcover with its blue I-A monogram of crossed sword and stylus, the hard chair backed against the foot of the bunk leaving a three-centimeter clearance for the gray flatness of a closet door.

Everything regulation and in its place.

But he could not put down the premonition that something here had changed . . . and dangerously.

Into that probing awareness, the hall door had banged open and Stetson had entered. The section chief wore his usual patched blue fatigues. His only badges of rank, golden I-A emblems on collar and uniform cap, appeared faintly corroded. Orne, wondering when the emblems had last seen polish, pushed that thought out of his mind. Stetson reserved all of his polish for his mind.

Behind Stetson like a pet on an invisible leash rolled a mechanocart piled high with cramtapes, microrecords and even some primitive books in stelaperm bindings. The cart trundled itself into the room, its wheels rumbling as it cleared the slideseal at the doorway.

Orne had focused on the cart, knowing it immediately as the object of his dread. He got to his feet, stared hard at Stetson. "What's this, Stet?"

Stetson pulled the chair from the foot of the bunk, sailed his cap onto the blanket. His dark hair straggled in an uncombed muss. His eyelids drooped. He said: "You've had enough assignments to know the trappings when you see them."

"Don't I have any say in that anymore? Orne asked.

"Well, now, things may've changed a bit and then again, maybe they haven't," Stetson said. "Besides, this concerns something you say you want."

"I'm getting married in three weeks," Orne said.

"Your wedding has been postponed," Stetson said. He held up a placating hand as Orne's face darkened. "Wait a bit. Postponed, nothing more."

"On whose orders?" Orne demanded.

"Well, now, Diana agreed to leave this morning on an assignment which the High Commissioner arranged for us."

"We were having dinner tonight!" Orne said, outraged.

"That's been postponed, too," Stetson said. "She sends her regrets. There's a visocube in that stuff on the cart—her regrets, her love and all of that, but she hopes you'll understand the purpose of her sudden departure."

Orne's voice came out in a growl: "What purpose?"

"The purpose of getting her out of your hair.

129

You're leaving for Amel in six days, not in six months, and there's a mountain of preparation before you're ready to go."

"You'd better explain a little more about Diana."

"She knows she would have wasted your time, distracted you, diverted attention which you absolutely require now. She's off to Franchi Primus to deliver some important personal information explaining to the Nathian underground there why they no longer are underground and why their handpicked candidate had to withdraw from the election so abruptly. She's perfectly safe and you can get married when you return from Amel."

"Provided you don't dream up some new emergency," Orne snarled.

"You're the ones who took the I-A oath," Stetson said. "She takes her orders just like the rest of us."

"Oh, this I-A is real fun," Orne growled. "I must recommend it whenever I find a likely young fellow looking for a job!"

"Amel, remember?" Stetson asked.

"But why so sudden?"

"Amel . . . well, Lew, Amel isn't quite the picnic ground you may have imagined."

"Not the . . . but it is *the* place for advanced psi training. You put through my application, didn't you?"

"Lew, that's not quite the way it works."

"Oh?"

"You don't apply to Amel, you are *summoned*."

"What's that supposed to mean?"

"There's only one way to go there if you're not on the approved list, a graduate or priest or some such.

130

That's as a student—summoned."

"And I've been summoned?"

"Yes."

"What if I refuse to go as a student?"

Hard lines formed beside Stetson's mouth. "You took an oath to the I-A. Do you remember it?"

"I'm going to rewrite that oath," Orne growled. "To the words *'I pledge my life and my sacred honor to seek out and destroy the seeds of war wherever they may be found'* let us add: *'and I will sacrifice anything and anybody in the process.'* "

"Not a bad addition," Stetson said. "Why don't you propose it when you get back?"

"*If* I get back!"

"Granted there's always *that* possibility," Stetson said. "But you have been summoned and the I-A wants desperately for you to accept."

"So that's why none of you questioned my request."

"That's part of it. Our Psi Branch confirmed that you were a genuine talent . . . and we had our hopes raised. We *want* someone of your caliber on Amel."

"Why? What's the I-A's interest in Amel? Never been a war anywhere near the place. The big shots are always afraid of offending their gods."

"Or their priests."

"I've never heard of anyone having trouble getting to Amel," Orne said.

"*We've* always had trouble."

"The I-A?"

"Yes."

"But our Psi Branch technicians were trained there."

"They are assigned to us out of Amel at Amel's insistence, not at ours. We've never been able to send a genuine investigative agent, trustworthy and dedicated, to Amel."

"You think the priests are cooking up something?"

"If they are, we're in trouble. How do we handle psi powers? What do we do to confine someone like that guy on Wessel who can jump to any planet in the universe without a ship? How do we deal with a man who can remove our instruments from within his flesh and without making an incision?"

"So you know about that, eh?"

"When our transceiver stopped giving us the noises of your surroundings and started giving us fish-gurgles, yes, we knew," Stetson said. "How'd you do that?"

"I don't know."

"And maybe you're telling me the truth," Stetson said.

"I just wished for it to happen," Orne said.

"You just wished! Maybe that's why you're going to Amel."

Orne nodded, dazzled by this thought. "It could be." But he still felt the premonition, not focused on the cart now, but going beyond it to Amel. "Are you sure it's me they've summoned?"

"We're sure and we're anxious."

"You haven't explained that, Stet."

Stetson sighed. "Lew, we just had confirmation on it this morning: At the next session of the Assembly there's going to be a motion to do away with the I-A, turning all of its functions over to Rediscovery & Reeducation."

"Oh, you must be joking."

"I'm not."

"Under Tyler Gemine and his Rah-Rah boys?"

"None other."

"Why . . . that political hack! Half our problems come from Rah-Rah stupidities. They've damn near bumbled us into another Rim War dozens of times. I thought Gemine was our target number one for removal from office."

"Mmmmm, hmmmm," Stetson agreed. "And at the next Assembly session, less than five months away now, this motion will come up and it has the full support of Amel's priesthood."

"*All* of the priesthood?"

"All of it."

"But that's asinine! I mean, look at the . . ."

"Do you have any doubts that religious heat can carry this motion through?" Stetson asked.

Orne shook his head. "But there are thousands of religious sects on Amel . . . millions, maybe. The Ecumenical Truce doesn't allow for . . ."

"The Truce doesn't say anything about not gunning for the I-A," Stetson said.

"But it doesn't fit, Stet. If the priests are after us, why would they invite *me* as a student at the same time?"

"Now you see why we're so anxious," Stetson said. "Nobody—repeat: *nobody!*—has ever before been able to put an agent onto Amel. Not the I-A. Not the old Marakian Secret Service. Not even the Nathians. All attempts have been met with polite ejection. No agent has ever gone farther than twenty meters from his landing site."

"What's on that cart you brought?" Orne asked.

"All of the stuff you were supposed to study for the next six months. You have six days."

"What provision will there be for getting me off if Amel goes sour?"

"None."

Orne stared at him incredulously. "None?"

"Our best information indicates that your training on Amel—they call it 'The Ordeal'—takes about six months. If there's no word from you within that limit, we'll make inquiries."

"Like: *'What've you done with his body?'* " Orne snarled. "Hell! There might not even be an I-A to make inquiry in six months!"

"There will, at least, be some concerned citizens, your friends."

"The *friends* who sent me in there!"

"I'm sure you see the necessity. Diana saw it."

"She knows all this?"

"Yes. She cried, but she saw the necessity and she went to Franchi Primus as ordered."

"I'm your last resort, eh?"

Stetson nodded. "We have to find out why the center of all religions has turned against us. We haven't a prayer, if you'll excuse the reference, of going in there and subduing them. We might try it, but it'd start religious uprisings all through the federation. Make the Rim Wars look like a game of ball at a girls' school."

"But you haven't ruled that out?"

"Of course not. But I'm not certain we could get enough volunteers to do the job. We never qualify personnel by religion. But I'm damned sure they'd qualify us if we made a move against Amel. That's touchy ground, Lew. No, we have to find out why! Maybe we can change whatever's bothering them. It's our only hope. Maybe they don't understand our . . ."

"What if they have plans for conquest by war, Stet? What then? A new faction could've come to power on Amel. Why not?"

Stetson looked sad. "If you could prove it . . ." He shrugged.

"What's first on the agenda?" Orne asked.

Stetson hooked a thumb at the cart. "Dive into that material. You'll be going back to the medics later today for a new and better psi amplifier."

"When do I go to the medics?"

"They'll come for you."

"Somebody's *always* coming for me," Orne muttered.

A universe without war involves critical-mass concepts as applied to human beings. Any immediate issue which might lead to war is always escalated to questions of personal value, to the complications of technological synergism, to questions of an ethico-religious nature, to which areas are open for counteraction and, inevitably, there remain the unknowns, omnipresent and likely of insidious complexity. The human situation as it relates to war can be likened to a multilinear looped feedback system in which nothing is unimportant.

—"War, the *Un*-possible,"
Chapter IV, *I-A Manual*

Evening light sent long shadows into Orne's hospital room at the I-A Medical Center. It was the quiet time between dinner and visiting hours. The pseudoperspective of the room had been closed in to produce surroundings of *restful security*. Decoracol stood at low-green, lights dim. The induction bandage felt bulky under his chin, but the characteristic quick-heal itching had not yet started.

Being in a hospital made Orne vaguely uneasy. He knew why. The smells and the sounds reminded him of all the months he'd spent creeping back from death after Sheleb. He recalled that Sheleb had been another planet where war could *not* originate.

Like Amel.

The door to his room slid aside, admitting a tall, bone-skinny tech officer with the forked lighting insig-

136

nia of Psi Branch at his collar. The door closed behind him.

Orne studied the man—an unknown face: birdlike with long nose, pointed chin, narrow mouth. The eyes made quick, darting movements. He lifted his right hand in a fluttery salute, leaned on the crossbar at the foot of Orne's bed.

"I'm Ag Emolirdo," he said, "head of Psi Branch. The Ag is for Agony."

Unable to move his head because of the induction bandage, Orne stared along his own nose down the length of the bed at Emolirdo. So this was the shy and mysterious chief of Psi in the I-A. The man radiated an aura of knowing confidence. He reminded Orne of a priest back on Chargon—another Amel graduate. The reminder made Orne uneasy. He said: "I've heard of you. How d'you do?"

"We're about to find out how I do," Emolirdo said. "I've reviewed your records. Fascinating. Are you aware that you may be a psi focus?"

"A what?" Orne tried to sit up, but the bandage restraints held him fast.

"Psi focus," Emolirdo said. "I'll explain in a moment."

"Please do that," Orne said. He found himself not liking Emolirdo's glib, all-knowing manner.

"You may consider this the beginning of your advanced training," Emolirdo said. "I decided to take it on myself. If you're what we suspect . . . well, it's extremely rare."

"How rare?"

"Well, the only others are lost behind the mythical veils of antiquity."

"I see. This psi focus thing, is that it?"

"That's what we call the phenomenon. If you are a psi focus, then you're . . . well, a god."

Orne blinked, sat in frozen shock. He felt the wheel of his life turning, the sense of his one-being aflame with a terrifying passion for existence. An overriding awareness churned within him, bringing up all the ancient functions of life for his review.

He thought: *Nothing can be excluded from life. It is all one thing.*

"You don't question that?" Emolirdo asked.

Orne swallowed, said: "I have questions, plenty of them."

"Ask."

"Why do you think I'm this . . . psi focus?"

Emolirdo nodded. "You appear to be an island of order in a disordered universe. Four times since you came to the attention of the I-A you've done the impossible. Any one of the problems you tackled could have led to ferment and perhaps general warfare. But you went in and brought order out of . . ."

"I did what I was trained to do, no more."

"Trained? By whom?"

"By the I-A, of course. That's a stupid question."

"Is it?" Emolirdo found a chair, sat down beside the bed, his head level with Orne's. "Let us take this in an orderly fashion, beginning with our articulation of life."

"I articulate life by living it," Orne said.

"Perhaps I should've said let us approach this from another viewpoint, just for the sake of definition. Life, as we understand it, represents a bridge between Order and Chaos. We define Chaos as raw energy, un-

138

tamed, available to anything that can subdue it and bring it into some form of Order. In this sense, Life becomes stored Chaos. Do you follow this?"

"I hear your words," Orne said.

"Ahhhh . . ." Emolirdo cleared his throat. "To restate the situation, Life feeds on Chaos, but must exist within Order. Chaos represents a background against which Life knows itself. This brings us to another background, the condition called *Stasis*. This can be compared to a magnet. Stasis attracts free energy to itself until the pressures of nonmovement, of nonadaptation, grow too great and an explosion occurs. Exploding, the forms once in Stasis go back to Chaos, to non-Order. One is left with the unavoidable observation that Stasis leads always to Chaos."

"That's dandy," Orne said.

Emolirdo frowned, then: "This rule holds true on both the chemical-inanimate level and the chemical-animate level. Ice, the stasis of water, explodes when brought into abrupt contact with extreme heat. The frozen society explodes when exposed to the heat of war or the burning contact of a strange new society. Nature abhors stasis."

"The way it abhors a vacuum," Orne said, speaking only in the hope of turning Emolirdo's words off. What was he driving at? "Why all of this talk of Chaos, Order, Stasis?"

"We think in terms of energy systems," Emolirdo said. "That is the psi approach. Do you have more questions?"

"You haven't explained anything," Orne said. "Words, just words. What's all this have to do with Amel or your suspicion that I'm a . . . psi focus?"

"As to Amel," Emolirdo said, "that appears to be a stasis that does not explode."

"Then maybe it isn't static."

"Very astute," Emolirdo said. "As to psi focus, that brings us to the problem of miracles. You have been summoned to Amel because we consider you a worker of miracles."

Pain stabbed through Orne's bandaged neck as he tried to turn his head. "Miracles?" he croaked.

"The understanding of psi represents the understanding of miracles," Emolirdo said in his didactic way. "There is a devil in anything we don't understand. Thus, miracles frighten us and fill us with feelings of insecurity."

"Such as that fellow who supposedly can jump from planet to planet without a ship," Orne said.

"He does do it," Emolirdo said. "It's another form of miracle to *wish* a device removed from your flesh and have that thing happen without harming you."

"What would happen if I wished you removed from my presence?" Orne asked.

An odd half smile flickered across Emolirdo's mouth. It was as though he had fought down an internal dispute on whether to cry or laugh and had solved it by doing neither. He said:

"That might be interesting, especially if I countered with a wish of my own."

Orne felt confused. He said: "I'm not tracking on this."

Emolirdo shrugged. "I am only saying that the study of psi is the study of miracles. We examine things that happen outside of recognized channels and in spite of accepted rules. The religious call such things miracles. We say we have encountered a psi phenomenon or the workings of a psi focus."

"Changing the label doesn't necessarily change the thing," Orne said. "I'm still not tracking."

"Have you ever heard about the miracle caverns on the ancient planets?" Emolirdo asked.

"I've heard the stories," Orne said.

"They are more than stories. Let me put it this way: Such places held concealed shapes, convolutions which projected out of our *apparent* universe. Except at such focus points, the raw and chaotic energies of the universe resist our desires for Order. But *at* such focal points, the raw energies of outer Chaos becomes richly available and can be tamed. By the very act of wishing it so, we mold this raw energy in unique new ways that defy our old rules." Emolirdo's eyes blazed. He seemed to be fighting for control of great inner excitement.

Orne wet his lips with his tongue. "Shapes?"

"The historical record is clear," Emolirdo said. "Men have bent wires, coiled them, carved bits of plastic, jumbled odd assortments of apparently unrelated objects . . . and miraculous things happen: A smooth metal surface becomes tacky as though smeared with glue. A man draws a pentagram on a certain floor and flames dance within it. Smoke curls from a strangely shaped bottle and suddenly obeys a man's will. These are all shapes, you see?"

"So?"

"Then there are certain living creatures, including humans, who conceal such a focus within themselves. They walk into . . . nothing and reappear light-years away. They have only to look at a person suffering from an incurable disease and the disease is cured. They raise the dead. They read minds."

Orne tried to swallow in a dry throat. Emolirdo spoke with such an air of confidence, of conviction. This was something beyond blind faith.

"But how does it help to call these things psi?" Orne asked.

"It takes these phenomena out of the realm of blind fear," Emolirdo said. He bent toward Orne's bedside light, thrust a fist between the light and the green wall at the head of the bed. "Look at this wall."

"I can't turn my head," Orne said.

"Sorry." Emolirdo withdrew his hand. "I was just making a shadow. You can imagine it. Let us say there were sentient beings confined to the flat plane of that wall and they saw the shadow of my fist. Could a genius among them imagine the shape which cast the shadow—a shape projected from outside of his dimension."

"It's an old, but interesting question," Orne said.

"What if a being within the wall plane fashioned a device which projected into our dimension?" Emolirdo asked. "He would be like the legendary blind men studying the elephant. His device would respond in ways that would not fit his dimensions. He'd have to guess at the new patterns, set up all sorts of optional postulates."

The skin of Orne's neck began to itch maddeningly under the bandage. He resisted the urge to probe there with a finger. Bits of Chargon's folklore flitted through his memory: the magicians of the forest, the little people who granted wishes in ways that made the wishers regret their desires, the cavern where the sick were cured.

The quick-heal itching lured his finger with almost irresistible force. He groped for a pill on his bedstand, gulped it, waited for the relief.

"You are thinking," Emolirdo said.

"You put a new psi amplifier in my neck," Orne said. "For what purpose?"

"It's an improved device for signaling the presence of psi activity," Emolirdo said. "It detects psi fields, the presence of focal shapes. It amplifies your latent abilities. It enables you better to resist psi-induced emotions and you can detect motivations in others through the reading of their emotions. It may enable you to detect dangers to your person when those dangers still are some distance away in time— prescience, if you will. I'm laying on some parahypnoidal sessions for you which will make these effects more understandable to you."

Orne felt a tingling in his neck, a vacant sensation in his stomach that wasn't related to hunger. Danger?

"You'll recognize the prescient sensation," Emolirdo said. "It'll come upon you as a peculiar kind of fear, perhaps mistaken for hunger. You'll sense a *lack* of something, perhaps inside you or in the air you're breathing. It's a very trustworthy signal of danger."

Orne felt the vacant sensation in his stomach. His skin was clammy with perspiration. The room's air tasted stale in his lungs. He wanted to reject the sensations and Emolirdo's suggestive conversation, but a fact named *Stetson* remained. Nobody in the I-A could be more coldly skeptical and Stet had said to go through with this.

There was also the matter of the transceiver he had *wished* from his flesh.

"You're a little pale," Emolirdo said.

Orne managed a tight smile. "I think I feel your prescient warning right now."

"Ahhhh. Describe your sensations."

Orne obeyed.

"Odd that it should happen so soon," Emolirdo said. "Can you identify a source for this danger?"

"You," Orne said. "And Amel."

Emolirdo pursed his lips. "Perhaps the psi training itself is dangerous to you. That *is* odd. Especially if you do turn out to be a psi focus."

When a wise man does not understand, he says: "I do not understand." The fool and the uncultured are ashamed of their ignorance. They remain silent when a question could bring them wisdom.

—Sayings of the ABBODS

There was no real excuse to wait on the transport's ramp any longer, Orne told himself. He had overcome the first staggering impact of Amel's psi forces. But the prescient awareness of peril remained with him like a sore tooth. He felt the heat, the heavy toga. Perspiration soaked him.

And his stomach said: *Wait.*

He took a half step toward the escalfield and the sense of vacancy within him expanded. His nostrils caught the acrid bite of incense, an odor so strong it rode over the oil-and-ozone dominance of the spaceport.

In spite of training and carefully nurtured agnosticism, he experienced a sensation of awe. Amel exuded an aura of magic that defied disbelief.

It's only psi, Orne told himself.

Chanting and keening sounds lifted like an aural fog from the religious warren. He felt memory fragments stirring from his childhood on Chargon: *the religious processions on holy days . . . the image of* Mahmud *glowering from the* kiblah *. . . the* azan *ringing out across the great square on the Day of Bairam—*

"Let no blasphemy occur, nor permit a blasphemer to live . . ."

Orne shook his head, thought: *Now'd be a great*

145

time to get religion and bow down to Ullua, *the star wanderer of the Ayrbs.*

The roots of his fear went deep. He tightened his belt, strode forward into the escalfield. The sense of danger remained, but grew no stronger.

The escalfield's feathery touch lowered him to the ground, disgorged him beside a covered walkway. It was hotter on the ground than on the ramp. Orne wiped perspiration from his forehead. A cluster of white-clad priests and students in aqua togas pressed into the thin shade of the covered walkway. They began to separate as Orne approached, leaving in pairs—a priest with each student.

One priest remained—tall, a thick body, a heavy feeling about him as though the ground would shake when he walked. *Another Chargon native?* Orne wondered. His head was shaved. Deep scratch lines patterned his face. Dark glowered from beneath overhanging gray brows.

"You Orne?" the priest rumbled.

Orne stepped under the walkway. "Yes." The priest's skin betrayed a yellow oiliness in the shadows.

"I am Bakrish," he said. He put slab hands on his hips, glared at Orne. "You missed the ceremony of lustration."

"I was told I could come down at my own time," Orne said.

"One of those, eh?" Bakrish said.

Something about the heavy figure, the glowering face reminded Orne of an I-A training sergeant on Marak. The memory restored Orne's sense of balance, brought a grin to his face.

146

"You find something amusing?" Bakrish demanded.

"This humble face reflects happiness to be in your presence upon Amel," Orne said.

"Yeah?"

"What'd you mean *one of those?*" Orne asked.

"You're one of those talents has to get his Amel balance," Bakrish said. "That's all. Come along." He turned, strode off under the walkway's cover, not looking to see if Orne followed.

Amel balance? Orne wondered.

He set off after Bakrish, found he had to force himself into a half trot to keep up.

No moving walks, no hopalongs, Orne thought. *This planet is primitive.*

The covered walk jutted like a long beak from a windowless low building of gray plastrete. Double doors opened into a dim hall that washed Orne with cool air. He noted, however, that the doors had to be opened by hand and one of them creaked. The hall echoed with their footsteps.

Bakrish led the way past rows of narrow cells without doors, some of them occupied by murmuring figures, some piled with strange equipment, some empty. At the end of the hall there was another door which opened into a room large enough to hold one small desk and two chairs. Pink light filled the room from concealed exciters. The place smelled of fungus. Bakrish crunched his frame into the chair behind the desk, motioned for Orne to take the other seat.

Orne obeyed, felt the stomach pangs of danger grow more acute.

147

Bakrish said: "As you know, we on Amel live under the Ecumenical Truce. The I-A intelligence service will have briefed you on the surface significance of this fact."

Orne concealed surprise at this turn in the conversation.

Bakrish said: "What you must understand now is that there is nothing unusual about my assignment as your guru."

"Why would it be thought unusual?" Orne asked.

"You are a follower of Mahmud and I am a Hynd and a *Wali* under divine protection. By the Truce, all of us serve the one God who has many names. You see?"

"No, I don't see."

"Hynd and Ayrb have a long tradition of enmity," Bakrish said. "Did you not know this?"

"I seem to have encountered a reference somewhere," Orne admitted. "My own attitude is that enmity leads to violence and violence leads to war. I have taken an oath to prevent this progression."

"Commendable, very commendable," Bakrish said. "When Emolirdo told us about you, we had to see for ourselves, of course. That's why you're here."

Orne thought: *So Stet was right; the Psi Branch spies for Amel.*

"You pose a fascinating problem," Bakrish said.

Orne set his face in a blank mask, probed with his newly awakened psi awareness for an emotion, a weakness, any clue to the peril he sensed here. He said: "I thought it was a simple matter of my coming here as a student."

"Nothing is truly simple," Bakrish said.

148

As Bakrish spoke, Orne felt his sense of danger dissipate, caught the priest glancing toward the doorway. Orne whirled, caught a flicker of robe and sight of a wheeled object being pulled away.

Bakrish said: "That's better. Now we have the tensor phase of your booster equipment. We can nullify it at will or destroy you with it."

Orne fought to control shock, wondered: *What kind of a bomb did Emolirdo have the medics plant in me?* He thought of wishing the devices out of his flesh, but wondered if he could do that on Amel. The thought of failure loomed as more dangerous than letting the matter ride temporarily. He said:

"I'm glad you found something to keep you busy."

"Do not sneer," Bakrish said. "We have no wish to destroy you. We want you to use the devices which were given to you. That is why you got them and were taught to use them."

Orne took two deep breaths. Psi training took over without conscious volition. He concentrated on the inner focus for calmness and it came like the wash of cool water. He became icy, observant, calm, sensitive to any psi force. And at the same time, thoughts blazed in his mind. This was not the pattern of events he had expected. Did they have him boxed?

"Have you any questions?" Bakrish asked.

Orne cleared his throat. "Yes. Will you help me to see the Abbod Halmyrach. I must find out why Amel is trying to destroy the . . ."

"All in its own time," Bakrish said.

"Where do I find the Abbod?"

"When the time comes, it will be arranged for you to see him. He is nearby and awaits these events with

149

great curiosity, I assure you."

"What events?"

"Your ordeal, of course."

"Of course. When you try to destroy me."

Bakrish appeared puzzled. "Believe me, my young friend, we have no desire to cause your destruction. We have merely taken necessary precautions. These are dangerous matters which engage our attentions."

"You said you could destroy me."

"Only under the most dire necessity. You must understand the two basic facts here now: You want to find out about us and we want to find out about you. The best way for both of us to accomplish this is for you to submit to your ordeal. You really have no choice."

"So you tell me!"

"I assure you."

"So I'm supposed to let you lead me along like a *grifka* going to the slaughterhouse. Either that or you destroy me."

"Bloody thoughts really are not suitable," Bakrish said. "Look upon this as I do: It is an interesting test."

"But just one of us is in danger."

"I would hardly say that," Bakrish said.

Orne felt anger surge through him. For this, he had suffered the postponement of his wedding, the ministrations of medics who very likely had been directed by a traitor to the I-A, had undergone the grinding psi course. For this!

"I'm going to find out what makes you tick," Orne grated, glaring at Bakrish. "When I do, I'm going to smash you."

Bakrish paled. His yellow skin appeared sickly. He

swallowed, shook his head. "You *must* be exposed to the mysteries," he murmured. "It is the only way we know."

Orne felt embarrassment at his burst of bravado, thought: *Why is this joker afraid? He's in the driver's seat here, but my threat frightened him. Why?*

"Do you submit to the ordeal?" Bakrish ventured.

Orne pushed himself back in the chair. "You said I have no choice."

"Truly, you have not."

"Then I submit. But the price is an interview with the Abbod!"

"Of course . . . if you survive."

We come from the All-One and return to the All-One. How can we keep anything from the Source that was and the End that is?
> —Sayings of the ABBODS

"He has arrived, Reverend Abbod," the priest said. "Bakrish is with him now."

The Abbod Halmyrach stood at a scribe's easel, his bare feet on an orange rug that matched his long robe. The room, its windows shuttered against Amel's glaring sunlight, appeared shadowy and archaic. Dim light came from ancient glowglobes which hovered in the upper corners of the room. There were wood walls and a fireplace with orange coals in it behind the Abbod. His narrow face with its long nose and thin-lipped mouth appeared calm, but the Abbod was acutely aware of his room, of the oily shadows on the wood walls, the scratching of the priest's sandals on the floor beyond the rug, the faint stirrings of the fire dying in the fireplace.

This priest reporting now, Macrithy, was one of the Abbod's most trusted observers, but the man's appearance—long black hair with deep sideburns framing a smoothly rounded face, the dark stovepipe suit and reversed white collar—bothered the Abbod. Macrithy looked too much like an historical illustration from accounts of the Second Inquisition. One did not, however, question religious accouterments which came under the freedoms of the Ecumenical Truce.

"I sensed his arrival," the Abbod said. He turned back to the easel, writing with pen on paper because it pleased him to keep the ancient ways alive. "There does not seem to be any doubt he is the one."

Macrithy said: "He has made the three transcendent steps, but there is no certainty he will survive his ordeal and discover you, who summoned him."

"To *discover* has many meanings," the Abbod said. "Have you read my brother's report?"

"I have read it, Reverend Abbod."

The Abbod looked up from his writing. "I saw the little green box, you know. I saw it in a vision in the instant before the Shriggar appeared to us. I also saw my brother and felt the transcendent influence on his emotions brought about by that moment. It fascinates me the way the prediction follows so precisely upon the Shriggar's words. It *tracks,* as they say." He returned to his writing.

"Reverend Abbod," Macrithy said, "the game of war, the city of glass and the time of politics are past. I have studied your account of the god making. It is now time for us to fear the consequences of our daring."

"And I *am* afraid," the Abbod said, not looking up.

"We all are," Macrithy said.

"But think of it," the Abbod said, putting a punctuation mark on his writing with a flourishing gesture. "This is our first *human!* What have we touched in the past—a mountain of Talies, the Speaking Stone of Krinth, the Mouse God on Old Earth, animate and inanimate elements of that ilk. Now, we have our first *human* god."

"There've been others," Macrithy said.

"But not of *our* making!"

"We may regret it," Macrithy muttered.

"Oh, I already do," the Abbod said. "But there's no changing that now, is there?"

The day is short and the work is great, and the workers are lazy, but the reward is large and our Master urges us to make haste.

—Writings of the
ABBOD HALMYRACH

"This is called 'the cell of meditation-on-faith,'" Bakrish said, gesturing toward the room whose door he had opened for Orne. "You are required to stretch out on the floor in there flat on your back. Do not sit or stand until I give permission. It is very dangerous."

"Why?" Orne leaned in, studied the room.

It was a high and narrow place. Walls, floor and ceiling appeared to be white stone veined by thin brown lines like insect tracks. Pale-white light, sourceless and flat as skimmed milk, filled the room. A smell of damp stone and fungus permeated the space.

"This is a psi machine of great potency," Bakrish said. "Flat on your back, you are relatively safe. Accept my word for it; I have seen the results of disbelief." He shuddered.

Orne cleared his throat. He felt cold. The vacant place in his stomach was a distended bag warning him of terrible peril. He said: "What if I refuse to go through with this?"

"Please," Bakrish said. "I am here to help you. It is more dangerous to turn back than it is to go ahead. Far more dangerous."

154

Orne sensed sincerity in the words, turned and met a pleading stare in the priest's dark eyes.

"Please," Bakrish said.

Orne took a deep breath, stepped into the cell. He felt a slight easing of the danger signal but it remained strong and insistent.

"Flat on your back," Bakrish said.

Orne stretched out on the floor. The stone chilled his back through the thick toga.

Bakrish said: "Once you start on your ordeal, the only way out is to go through it. Remember that."

"Have you been through this?" Orne asked. He felt oddly silly stretched out on the floor. Bakrish, seen from this angle, appeared tall and powerful in the doorway.

"But of course," Bakrish said.

If his psi awareness could be trusted, Orne thought he detected profound sympathy at the priest's emotive base.

"What's at the other end of this ordeal?" Orne asked.

"That's for each to discover for himself."

"Is it really more dangerous for me to back out now?" Orne asked. He raised himself on one elbow. "I think you're just using me, maybe in an experiment."

A sense of regret radiated from Bakrish. He said: "When the scientist sees that his experiment has failed, he is not necessarily barred from further attempts . . . using new equipment. You truly have no choice. Flat on your back now; it is safest for you."

Orne obeyed, said: "Then let's get on with it."

"As you command," Bakrish said. He stepped back

and the doorway vanished. No sign of it remained in the wall.

Orne felt his throat go dry, studied his cell. It appeared to be about four meters long, two meters wide, some ten meters high. The mottled stone ceiling was blurred, though, and he thought the room could be higher. The pale illumination could have been designed to confuse the senses.

The prescient warning remained within him, a tense reminder of peril.

Abruptly, Bakrish's voice filled the room, sourceless and booming. It was everywhere, all around and within Orne. Bakrish said: "You are within the psi machine. It encloses you. The ordeal you are entering is ancient and it is exacting. It is to test the quality of your faith. Failure means loss of your life, loss of your soul . . . or of both."

Orne clenched his hands into fists. Perspiration bathed his palms. He felt an abrupt increase in background psi activity.

Faith?

He found himself remembering his ordeal in the crechepod and the dream that once had plagued him. *Gods are made, not born.* In the crechepod he had rebuilt his own being, coming back from death, discarding old ways, old nightmares.

A test of faith?

In what could he possibly have faith? In himself? He recalled the time of the crechepod and his sense of questioning. He had questioned the I-A then, awareness churning. Somewhere within himself he had sensed an ancient function, a thing of archaic tendencies.

He remembered then his one-part definition of existence: *I am one being. I exist. That is enough. I give life to myself.*

There was something to be taken on faith.

Again, the voice of Bakrish boomed in the cell: "Immerse your selfdom in the mystical stream, Orne. What can you possibly fear?"

Orne sensed the psi pressures focused upon him, all of the evidences of deep and hidden intent. He said: "I like to know where I'm going, Bakrish."

"Sometimes we go for the sake of going," Bakrish said.

"Nuts!"

"When you press the stud which turns on a room's lights you act on faith," Bakrish said. "You have faith that there will be light."

"I have faith in past experience," Orne said.

"What about the first time, the time of no experience?"

"I must've been surprised."

"Do you possess awareness of every experience available to humankind?" Bakrish asked.

"I guess not."

"Then prepare yourself for surprises. I must tell you now that no lighting mechanism exists in your cell. The light you see exists because you desire it and for no other reason."

"What . . ."

Darkness engulfed the room, Stygian and sense-denying. His prescient awareness of peril clamored.

Bakrish's husky whisper filled the darkness: "Have faith, my student."

Orne fought down the urgent desire to leap up and

dash toward the doorwall, to pound on it. There had to be a doorway there! But he sensed the matter-of-fact grimness in the priest's warning. Death lay in flight. There was no turning back.

A smoky glow appeared high up in the cell and coiled downward toward Orne. *Light?* It did not fit his definition of light, but appeared to have a life of its own, an inward source of glowing.

Orne brought his right hand in front of his eyes. He could see the hand only in outline against the glowing. The radiance cast no light into the cell. The sense of pressure increased with each heartbeat.

He thought: *It became dark when I doubted.*

Did the milky light that had been in the cell represent an opposition to darkness, a fear of darkness?

Shadowless illumination flickered into being throughout the cell, but it was dimmer than it had been at first, and a black cloud boiled near the ceiling where the smoky radiance had been. The cloud beckoned like the outer darkness of deepest space.

Orne stared at the cloud, terrified by it.

The sense-denying darkness returned.

Once more, the smoky radiance glowed near the ceiling.

Prescient fear screamed in Orne. He closed his eyes in the effort to put down that fear and to concentrate. As his eyes closed, the fear eased. His eyes snapped open in shock.

Fear!

The ghostly glowing dipped nearer.

Eyes closed!

The sense of immediate peril retreated.

He thought: *Fear equals darkness. The darkness beckons even when there is light.* He calmed his breathing pattern, concentrated on the inward focus. *Faith? Did that mean* blind *faith?*

Fear brought the darkness. What did they want of him?

I exist. That is enough.

He forced his eyes to open, stared upward into the cell's lightless void. The dangerous glowing coiled toward him. Even in utter darkness there was false light. It was not real light because he could not see by it. It was *antilight.* He could detect its presence anywhere, even in darkness.

Orne recalled a time long ago in his Chargon childhood, a time of darkness in his own bedroom. Moon shadows had been translated into monsters. He had pressed his eyes tightly closed, fearful that he would see things too horrible to contemplate if he opened them.

False light.

Orne stared upward at the coiling radiance. Did false light equal false faith? The radiance coiled backward onto itself. Did the utter darkness equal utter absence of faith? The radiance winked out.

Is it enough to have faith in my own existence? Orne wondered.

The cell remained dark and dangerous. He smelled the stone dampness. Creeping sounds infected the darkness—claw scrabbles, hisses and scratches, slitherings and squeaks. Orne invested the sounds with every shape of terror his imagination could produce: poisonous lizards, insane monsters, deadly snakes, fang-toothed crawling things out of nightmares. The sense of peril enfolded him. He lay suspended in it.

Bakrish's hoarse whisper snaked through the darkness: "Are your eyes open, Orne?"

Orne's lips trembled with the effort to answer: "Yes."

"What do you see?"

The question produced an image which danced on the black field in front of Orne. He saw Bakrish in an eerie red light, face contorted with agony, his body leaping, capering . . .

"What do you see?" Bakrish demanded.

"I see you. I see you in Sadun's inferno."

"In the hell of Mahmud?"

"Yes. Why do I see that?"

"Do you not prefer the light, Orne?" There was terror in Bakrish's voice.

"Why do I see you in hell, Bakrish?"

"I beg of you, Orne! Choose the light. Have faith!"

"But why do I see you in . . ."

Orne broke off, caught by the sensation that something had peered inside him with heavy deliberation. It had checked his thoughts, examined his vital processes and every unspoken desire, weighted his *soul* and cataloged it.

A new kind of awareness remained. Orne knew that if he willed it, Bakrish would be cast into the deepest torture pit of Mahmud's nightmares.

He had only to wish it.

Why not? he asked himself.

Then again: *Why?*

Who was he to make such a decision? Had Bakrish earned eternity of Mahmud's hate? Was Bakrish the one who had set out to destroy the I-A? Bakrish was a minion, a mere priest. *The Abbod Halmyrach, however . . .*

Groaning and creaking filled the cell. A tongue of flame leaped out of the darkness above Orne, a fiery lance poised and aimed, casting a ruddy glow on the cell's walls.

Prescient warning clawed at Orne's stomach.

Who was a proper target for Mahmud's fanatical violence? If the wish were made, would it strike only one target? What of the one who wished this thing? Was a backlash possible?

Would I join the Abbod in hell?

Orne possessed the certain awareness that he could in this instant do a dangerous and devilish thing. He could cast a fellow human into eternal agony.

What human and why?

Was possession of an ability the license to use it? He found himself revolted by the momentary temptation to do this thing. *No human deserved that. No human ever had deserved it.*

I exist, he thought. *That is enough. Do I fear myself?*

The dancing flame winked out of existence. It left the darkness and its hissings, scrabblings, slitherings.

Orne felt his own fingernails trembling against the floor. Realization swept over him. *Claws!* He stilled his hands, laughed aloud as the claw sound stopped. He felt his feet writhing with involuntary efforts at flight. He stilled his feet. The suggestive slithering vanished.

Only the hissing remained.

He realized it was his own breath fighting its way through his clenched teeth.

Laughter convulsed him.

Light!

Brilliant light flared in the cell.

With sudden perversity, Orne rejected the light and darkness returned—a warm and quiet darkness.

He knew the psi machine around him was responding to his innermost wishes, to those wishes uncensored by doubting consciousness, to those wishes in which he had faith.

I exist.

Light was his for the wishing, but he had chosen this darkness. In the sudden release of tensions, Orne ignored Bakrish's warning, got to his feet. Being on his back had made it easier to understand his own innermost passivity, the assumptions and acceptances which clouded his being. The clouds were gone now. Orne smiled into the darkness, called out: "Bakrish, open the door."

A psi probe peered into Orne, slow and ponderous. He recognized Bakrish in it.

"You can see I have faith," Orne said. "Open up."

"Open it yourself," Bakrish said.

Orne willed it: *Show me Bakrish.*

A sandy scraping filled the cell Light fanned inward from the side as the entire wall opened. Orne looked out at Bakrish, a shadow framed against light like a robed statue.

The Hynd stepped forward, jerked to a halt as he saw Orne standing in darkness.

"Did you not prefer the light, Orne?"

"No."

"But you're standing, unafraid of my warning. You must have understood the test."

"I understood," Orne agreed. "The psi machine obeys my uncensored will. That's faith, the uncensored will."

"You understand and *still* choose the dark?"

"Does that bother you, Bakrish?"

"Yes."

"For the moment, I find that useful," Orne said.

"I see." Bakrish bowed his shaven head. "I thank you for sparing me."

"You know about that?" Orne was surprised.

"I felt the flames and the heat. I smelled the burning. I sensed my own screams of agony." Bakrish shook his head. "The life of a guru on Amel is not an easy one. There exist too many possibilities."

"You were safe," Orne said. "I censored my will."

"Therein lies the most enlightened degree of faith," Bakrish murmured. He brought up his hands, palms together and once more bowed to Orne.

Orne stepped out of the dark cell. "Is that all there is to my ordeal?"

"Oh, that was merely the initial step," Barkrish said. "There are seven steps: the test of faith, the test of the miracle and its two faces, the test of dogma and ceremony, the test of ethics, the test of religious ideal, the test of service to life, and the test of the personal mystique. They do not necessarily fall in that order and sometimes are not distinctly separated."

Orne tasted a sense of exhilaration, sensed that his prescient awareness of peril had receded. He said: "Let's get on with it."

Bakrish sighed, said: "Holy Rama defend me."

Then: "Very well, the two faces of the miracle, that is indicated next."

The sense of peril came alive once more in Orne. He fought to ignore it, thinking: *I have faith in myself. I can conquer my fear.*

Angrily, Orne said: "The sooner we get through this the sooner I see the Abbod. That's why I'm here."

"Is that the only reason?" Bakrish asked.

Orne hesitated, then: "Of course not. But he's the one who's putting the heat on the I-A. When I've solved all of your riddles, I'll still have him to solve."

"He is the one who summoned you, that is true," Bakrish said.

"I thought of casting him into hell," Orne said.

Bakrish paled. "The Abbod?"

"Yes."

"Rama, guard us!"

"Lewis Orne guard you," Orne said. "Let's get on with it."

The pattern of massive lethal violence, that phenomenon we call war, is maintained by a guilt-fear-hate syndrome which is transmitted much in the manner of a disease by social conditioning. Although lack of immunity to this disease is a very human thing, the disease itself is not a necessary and natural condition of human existence. Among those conditioned patterns which transmit the war virus you will find the following—the justification of past mistakes, feelings of self-righteousness and the need to maintain such feelings . . .

—UMBO STETSON,
Lectures to the Antiwar College

Bakrish stopped before a heavy bronze door at the end of a long hall down which he had guided Orne. The priest turned an ornate handle cast in the form of a sunburst with long projecting rays. He threw his shoulder against the door and it creaked open.

He said: "We generally don't come this way. These two tests seldom follow each other in the same ordeal."

Orne stepped through the door after Bakrish, found himself in a gigantic room. Stone and plastrete walls curved away to a domed ceiling far above them. Slit windows in the high curve of the ceiling admitted thin shafts of light that glittered downward through gilt dust. Orne's gaze followed the light down to its focus on a straight wall barrier about twenty meters high and forty or fifty meters long. The wall was chopped off and appeared incomplete in the middle of the im-

165

mense room, dwarfed by the space around it.

Bakrish circled around behind Orne, closed the heavy door. He nodded toward the barrier wall. "We go there." He led the way; Orne followed.

Their slapping sandals created an oddly delayed echo. The smell of damp stone was a bitter taste in Orne's nostrils. He glanced left, saw evenly spaced doors around the room's perimeter—bronze doors appearing identical to the one they had entered. Looking over his shoulder, he tried to pick out their door. It was lost in the ring of sameness.

Bakrish came to a halt about ten meters from the center of the odd barrier wall. Orne stopped beside him. The wall's surface appeared to be smooth gray plastrete, featureless, but menacing. Orne felt his prescient fear increase as he stared at the wall. The fear came like the surging and receding of waves on a beach. Emolirdo had interpreted this as *Infinite possibilities in a situation basically perilous.*

What was there in a blank wall to produce such warning?

Bakrish glanced at Orne. "Is it not true, my student, that one should obey the orders of his superiors?" The priest's voice carried a hollow echo in the room's immensity.

Orne coughed to clear the rasping dryness of his throat. "If the orders make sense and the ones who give them are *truly* superior, I suppose so. Why do you ask?"

"Orne, you were sent here as a spy, as an agent of the I-A. By rights, anything that happens to you here is the concern of your superiors and no concern of ours."

166

Orne tensed. "What're you driving at?"

Sweat gleamed on Bakrish's forehead. He looked down at Orne, the dark eyes glistening. "These machines terrify us sometimes, Orne. They are unpredictable in any absolute sense. Anyone who comes within their field can be subjected to their power."

"Like back there when you were hanging on the edge of the inferno?"

"Yes." Bakrish shuddered.

"But you still want me to go through with this?"

"You must. It is the only way you can accomplish what you were sent here to do. You could not stop, you do not want to stop. The wheel of the Great Mandala is turning."

"I was not sent here," Orne said. "The Abbod summoned me. I am *your* concern, Bakrish. Otherwise you would not be here with me. Where is your own faith?"

Bakrish pressed his palms together, placed them in front of his nose and bowed. "The student teaches the guru."

"Why do you voice these fears?" Orne asked.

Bakrish lowered his hands. "It is because you still suspect us and fear us. I reflect your own fears. This emotion leads to hate. You saw that in your first test. But in the test you are about to undergo, hate represents the supreme danger."

"To whom, Bakrish?"

"To yourself, to all of those you may influence. Out of this test comes a rare kind of understanding, for it is . . ."

He broke off at a scraping sound behind them. Orne turned, saw two acolytes depositing a heavy, square-

167

armed chair on the floor facing the barrier wall. They cast frightened glances at Orne, scurried away toward one of the bronze doors.

"They fear me," Orne said, nodding toward the door where the acolytes had fled. "Does that mean they hate me?"

"They stand in awe of you," Bakrish said. "They are prepared to offer you reverence. It would be difficult for me to say how much of awe and reverence represents suppressed hate."

"I see."

Bakrish said: "I merely follow orders here, Orne. I beg of you not to hate me nor to hate anyone. Do not harbor hate during this test."

"Why do those two stand in awe of me and prepared to reverence me?" Orne asked, his gaze still on the door where the acolytes had gone.

"Word of you has gone forth," Bakrish said. "They know this test. The fabric of our universe is woven into it. Many things hang in the balance here when a potential psi focus is concerned. The possibilities are ininfinite."

Orne probed for Bakrish's motives. The priest obviously sensed the probe. He said: "I am terrified. Is that what you wanted to know?"

"Why?"

"In *my* ordeal, this test almost proved fatal. I had sequestered a core of hate. This place clutches at me even now." He shivered.

Orne found the priest's fear unsteadying.

Bakrish said: "I would deem it a favor if you would pray with me now."

"To whom?" Orne asked.

"To any force in which we have faith," Bakrish said. "To ourselves, to the One God, to each other. It does not matter; only it helps if we pray."

Bakrish clasped his hands, bowed his head.

After a moment's hesitation, Orne imitated him.

Which is the better: a good friend, a good heart, a good eye, a good neighbor, a good wife, or the understanding of consequences? It is none of these. A warm and sensitive soul which knows the worth of fellowship and the price of the individual dignity—this is best.

—BAKRISH as a student to his guru

"Why did you choose Bakrish to guide him in the ordeal?" Macrithy asked the Abbod.

They stood in the Abbod's study, Macrithy having returned to report that Orne had passed the first test. A smell of sulfur dominated the room and it seemed oppressively hot to Macrithy, although the fire had died in the fireplace.

The Abbod bowed his head over the standing easel, spoke without turning and without observing that Macrithy had coveted this honor for himself.

"I chose Bakrish because of something he said when he was my student," the Abbod murmured. "There are times, you know, when even a god needs a friend."

"What's that smell in here?" Macrithy asked. "Have you been burning something odd in the fireplace, Reverend Abbod?"

"I have tested my own soul in hellfire," the Abbod said, knowing that his tone betrayed his dissatisfaction with Macrithy. To soften this, he added: "Pray for me, my dear friend. Pray for me."

The teacher who does not learn from his students does not teach. The student who sneers at his teacher's true knowledge is like one who chooses unripe grapes and scorns the sweet fruit of the vine which has been allowed to ripen in its own time.

—Sayings of the ABBODS

"You must sit in that chair," Bakrish said when they had finished praying.

He indicated the squat, ugly shape facing the barrier wall.

Orne looked at the chair, noted an inverted metallic bowl fitted to swing over the seat. There was prescient tension in that chair. Orne felt his heartbeats pumping pressure into this moment.

"Sometimes we go for the sake of going." The words rang in his memory and he wondered who had

said them. The great wheel was turning.

Orne crossed to the chair, sat down.

In the act of sitting, he felt the sense of peril come to full surge within him. Metal bands leaped from concealed openings in the chair, pinned his arms, circled his chest and legs. He surged against them, twisting.

"Do not struggle," Bakrish warned. "You cannot escape."

"Why didn't you warn me I'd be pinned here?" Orne demanded.

"I did not know. Truly. The chair is part of the psi machine and, through you, has a life of its own. Please, Orne, I beg of you as a friend: do not struggle, do not hate us. Hate magnifies your danger manyfold. It could cause you to fail."

"Dragging you down with me?"

"Quite likely," Bakrish said. "One cannot escape the consequences of his hate." He glanced around the enormous room. "And I once hated in this place." He sighed, moved behind the chair and shifted the inverted bowl until it could be lowered over Orne's head. "Do not move suddenly or try to jerk away. The microfilament probes within this bowl will cause you great pain if you do."

Bakrish lowered the bowl.

Orne felt something touch his scalp in many places, a crawling and tickling sensation. "What is this thing?" he asked, his voice echoing oddly in his ears. And he wondered suddenly: *Why am I going through with this? Why do I take their word for everything?*

"This is one of the great psi machines," Bakrish said. He adjusted something on the back of the chair. Metal clicked. "Can you see the wall in front of you?"

171

Orne stared straight ahead under the lip of the bowl. "Yes."

"Observe that wall," Bakrish said. "It can manifest your most latent urges. With this machine, you can bring about miracles. You can call forth the dead, do many wonders. You may be on the brink of a profound mystical experience."

Orne tried to swallow in a dry throat. "If I wanted my father to appear here he would?"

"He is deceased?"

"Yes."

"Then it could happen."

"It would really be my father, alive . . . himself?"

"Yes. But let me caution you. The things you see here will not be hallucinations. If you are successful in calling forth the dead, what you call forth will be that dead person and . . . something more."

The back of Orne's right arm tingled and itched. He longed to scratch it. "What do you mean *more?*"

"It is a living paradox," Bakrish said. "Any creature manifested here through your will must be invested with your psyche as well as its own. Its matter will impinge upon your matter in ways which cannot be predicted. All of your memories will be available to whatever living flesh you call forth."

"My memories? But . . ."

"Hear me, Orne. This is important. In some cases, your *creates* may fully understand their duality. Others will reject your half of the creation out of hand. They may not have the capacity to straddle this dependence. Some of them may even lack sentience."

Orne felt the fear driving Bakrish's words, sensed the sincerity, and thought: *He believes this.* That didn't make all of this true, but it added a peculiar weight to the priest's words.

"Why have I been trapped in this chair?" Orne asked.

"I am not sure. Perhaps it was important that you not run away from yourself." Bakrish put a hand on Orne's shoulder, pressed gently. "I must leave now, but I will pray for you. May grace and faith guide you."

Orne heard a swishing of robes as the priest strode away. A door banged with a hollow sharpness which lost itself in the giant room. Infinite loneliness penetrated Orne.

Presently, a faint humming like a distant bee sound grew audible. The psi amplifier in Orne's neck tugged painfully, and he felt the flare of psi forces around him. The barrier wall blinked alive, became a rich and glassy green. It began to crawl with iridescent purple lines. They squirmed and writhed like countless glowing worms trapped in a viscid green aquarium.

Orne drew in a shuddering breath. Fear hammered at him. The crawling purple lines held a hypnotic fascination. Some appeared to waft out of the wall toward him. The shape of Diana's face glowed momentarily among the lines. He tried to hold the image, saw it melt away.

I don't want her here in this dangerous place, he thought.

Shapes of deformity squirmed across the wall. They coalesced abruptly into the outline of a Shriggar, the saw-toothed lizard Chargonian mothers invoked to frighten their children into obedience. The image took

173

on more substance. It developed scaly yellow plates and stalk eyes.

Time slowed to a grinding, creeping pace for Orne. He thought back to his Chargon childhood, to the terror memories, told himself: *But even then the Shriggar were extinct. My great-great-grandfather saw the last specimen.*

Memories persisted, driving him down a long corridor full of empty echoes that suggested insanity, drugged gibbering. Down . . . down . . . down . . . He recalled childish laughter, a kitchen, his mother as a young woman. There were his sisters screaming derisively as he cowered, ashamed. He had been three years old and he had come running into the house to babble in terror that he had seen a Shriggar in the deep shadows of the creek gully.

Laughing girls! Hateful little girls! "He thinks he saw a Shriggar!" "Hush now, you two." Amusement, even there in his mother's voice. He knew it now.

On the green wall, the Shriggar outline bulged outward. One taloned foot extended itself to the floor. The Shriggar stepped fully from the wall. It was twice as tall as a man and with stalked eyes swiveling right, left . . .

Orne jerked his awareness out of the memories, felt painful throbbing as his head movement disturbed the microfilament probes.

Talons scratched on the floor as the Shriggar took three investigative steps away from the wall.

Orne tasted the sourness of terror in his mouth. He thought: *My ancestors were hunted by such a creature.* The panic was in his genes. He recognized this as every sense focused on the nightmare lizard.

174

Yellow scales rasped with every breath the thing took. The narrow, birdlike head twisted to one side, lowered. Its beak mouth opened to reveal a forked tongue and sawteeth.

Primordial instinct pressed Orne back in his chair. He smelled the stink of the creature—sickly sweet with overtones of sour cream and swamp.

The Shriggar bobbed its head and coughed: "Chunk!" Stalk eyes moved, centered on Orne. One taloned foot lifted and it plunged into motion toward the man trapped in the chair. The high-stepping lope stopped about four meters away. The lizard cocked its head to one side while it examined Orne.

The beast stink of the thing almost overpowered Orne's senses. He stared up at it, aware of painful constriction across his chest, the probing eyes.

The green wall behind the Shriggar continued to wriggle with iridescent purple lines. The movement was a background blur on Orne's vision. He could not shift his focus from the lizard. The Shriggar ventured closer. Orne smelled the fetid swamp ooze on its breath.

This had to be hallucination, Orne told himself. *I don't care what Bakrish said: This is hallucination. Shrigger are extinct.* Another thought blinked at him in the sway of the lizards terrible beak: *The priests of Amel could've bred zoo specimens. How does anyone know what's been done here in the name of religion?*

The Shriggar cocked its head to the other side, moved its stalked eyes to within a meter of Orne's face. Something else solidified at the green wall. Orne moved only his eyes to discover what lay in this new movement.

Two children dressed in scanty sun aprons skipped onto the stone floor. Their footsteps echoed. Childish giggling rang in the vast emptiness of the domed room. One child appeared to be about five years old, the other slightly older—possibly eight. They betrayed the Chargon heaviness of body. The older child carried a small bucket and a toy shovel. They stopped, looked around them in sudden confused silence.

The smaller one said: "Maddie, where are we?"

At the sound, the Shriggar turned its head, bent its stalked eyes toward the children.

The older child shrieked.

The Shriggar whirled, talons scratching and slipping, lunged into its high-stepping lope.

In horrified shock, Orne recognized the children: his two sisters, the ones who'd laughed at his fearful cries on that long-ago day. It was as though he had brought this incident into being for the sole purpose of venting his hate, inflicting upon these children the thing they had derided.

"Run!" he shouted. "Run!"

But there was no moving the two children from their frozen terror.

The Shriggar swooped upon the children, blocking them from Orne's view. There was a childish shriek which was cut off with abrupt finality. Unable to stop, the lizard hit the green wall and melted into it, became wriggling lines.

The older child lay sprawled on the floor still clutching her bucket and toy shovel. A red smear marked the stones beside her. She stared across the room at Orne, slowly got to her feet.

176

This can't be real, Orne thought. *No matter what Bakrish said.*

He stared at the wall, expecting the Shriggar to reappear, but aware the beast had served its purpose. Without words, it had spoken to him. He saw that it had really been a part of himself. That was what Bakrish had meant. *That thing was my beast.*

The child began walking toward Orne, swinging her bucket. Her right hand clutched the toy shovel. She glared fixedly at Orne.

It's Maddie, he thought. *It's Maddie as she was. But she's a grown woman now, married and with children of her own. What have I created?*

Flecks of sand marked the child's legs and cheeks. One of her red braids hung down partly undone. She appeared angry, shivering with a child's fury. She stopped about two meters from Orne.

"You did that!" she accused.

Orne shuddered at the madness in the child voice.

"You killed Laurie!" she accused. "It was you."

"No, Maddie, no," Orne whispered.

She lifted the bucket, hurled its contents at him. He shut his eyes, felt sand deluge his face, pelt the bowl on his head. It ran down his cheeks, fell on his arms, his chest, his lap. He shook his head to dislodge the sand on his cheeks, and pain coursed through him as the movement disrupted the microfilaments connected to his scalp.

Through slitted eyes, Orne saw the dancing lines on the green wall leap into wild motion—bending, twisting, flinging. Orne stared at the green and purple frenzy through a red haze of pain. He remembered the

177

priest's warning that any life he called forth here would contain his own psyche as well as its own.

"Maddie," he said, "please try to under—"

"You tried to get into my head!" she screamed. "I pushed you out and you can't get back!"

Bakrish had said it: *Others may reject your half of the creation out of hand.* Child Maddie had rejected him because her eight-year-old mind could not accept such an experience.

Realizing this, Orne recognized that he was accepting this occurrence as reality and not as hallucination. He thought: *What can I say to her? How can I undo this?*

"I'm going to kill you!" Maddie screamed.

She hurled herself at him, the toy shovel swinging. Light glinted from the tiny blade. It slashed down on his right arm and pain exploded there. Blood darkened the sleeve of his toga.

Orne felt himself caught up in nightmare. Words leaped to his lips: "Maddie! Stop that or God will punish you!"

She drew back, preparing herself for a new assault.

More movement at the wall caught Orne's attention. A white-robed figure in a red turban came striding out of the wall: a tall man with gleaming eyes, the face of a tortured ascetic—long gray beard parted in the Sufi style.

Orne whispered the name: *"Mahmud!"*

A gigantic tri-di of that face and figure dominated the rear wall of the inner mosque Orne had attended on Chargon.

God will punish you!

Orne remembered standing beside an uncle, staring

178

up at that image in the mosque, bowing to it.

Mahmud strode up behind the child, caught her arm as she started another blow with the shovel. She twisted, struggling, but he held her, turning her arm slowly, methodically. A bone snapped. The child screamed and screamed and . . .

"Don't!" Orne protested.

Mahmud had a low, rumbling voice. He said: "One does not command God's agent to stop His just punishments." He lifted the child by the hair, caught up the fallen shovel, slashed it across her neck.

The screaming stopped. Blood spurted over his gown. He let the now limp figure fall to the floor, dropped the shovel, faced Orne.

Nightmare! Orne thought. *This has to be a nightmare!*

"You think this is a nightmare," Mahmud rumbled.

Orne remembered what Bakrish had said: If this creature were real, it could think with his memories. He rejected this thought. "You *are* a nightmare."

"Your creation has done its work," Mahmud said. "It had to be disposed of, you know. It was embodied by hate and not by love. You were warned about that."

Orne felt guilty, sickened and angry. He recalled that this test involved understanding miracles. "Was this supposed to be a miracle?" he asked. *"This* was a profound mystical experience?"

"You should've talked to the Shriggar," Mahmud said. "It would've discussed cities of glass, the meanings of war, politics and that sort of thing. I will be more demanding. For one thing, I wish to know what you believe constitutes a miracle."

179

An air of suspense enclosed Orne. Prescient fear sucked at his vitals.

"What is a miracle?" Mahmud demanded.

Orne felt his heart hammering. He had difficulty focusing on the question, stammered: "Are you really an agent of God?"

"Quibbles and labels!" Mahmud barked. "Haven't you learned yet about labels? The universe is one thing! We cannot cut it into pieces with our puny expediencies. The universe exists beyond the labels!"

A tingling sense of madness prickled through Orne. He felt himself balanced on the edge of chaos. *What is a miracle?* he wondered. He recalled Emolirdo's didactic words: *chaos . . . order . . . energy. Psi equals miracles.*

Words, more words.

Where was his faith?

I exist, he thought. *That is enough.*

"I am a miracle," he said.

"Ohhh, very good," Mahmud said. "Psi focus, eh? Energy from chaos shaped into duration. But is a miracle good or evil?"

Orne took a shuddering breath. "I've always heard that miracles are good, but they really don't have to be good or evil. Good and evil relate to motives. Miracles just *are*."

"Men have motives," Mahmud said.

"Men can be good or evil by any definitions they want," Orne said. "Where's the miracle in that?"

Mahmud stared down his nose at Orne. "Are you good or evil?"

Orne returned the stare. Winning through this test in his ordeal had taken on a profound meaning for him. He accepted now that this Mahmud was real. What was the prophet trying to make him say?

"How can I be good or evil to myself?" Orne asked.

"Is that your answer?"

Orne felt danger in the question, said: "You're trying to get me to say that men create gods to enforce their definitions of good and evil!"

"Oh? Is that the source of godliness? Come now, my friend. I know your mind; you have the answer in it."

Am I good or evil? Orne asked himself. He forced his attention onto the question, but it was like wading upstream in a swift river. His thoughts twisted and turned, showed a tendency to scatter. He said:

"I'm . . . if I'm one with all the universe, then I am God. I am creation. I am *the* miracle. How can that be good *or* evil?"

"What is it about creation?" Mahmud demanded. "Answer me that! Stop evading!"

Orne swallowed, recalled the nightmare sequence of this test. *Creation?* And he wondered if the great psi machine amplified the energy humans called religion.

He thought: *Bakrish said I could bring the dead to life here. Religion's supposed to have a monopoly on that. But how do I separate psi from religion from creation? The original Mahmud's been dead for centuries. If I have re-created him, how do his questions relate to me?*

And there was always the possibility this whole thing was some form of hallucination despite the peculiar sense of reality of it.

"You *know* the answer," Mahmud insisted.

Pressed to his limits, Orne said: "By definition, a

181

creation may act independently of its creator. You are independent of me even though you partake of me. I have cast you loose, given you your freedom. How can I judge you, then? You cannot be good or evil except in your own eyes. Nor can I!" Exultantly, he demanded: "Am I good or evil, Mahmud?"

"Thou sayest it for thyself and, thereby, are reborn an innocent," Mahmud said. "Thou hast learned thy lesson and I bless thee for it."

The robed figure bent, lifted the dead child. There was an odd tenderness in Mahmud's motions. He turned away, marched back into the writhing green wall. Silence blanketed the room. The dancing purple lines became almost static, moved in viscous torpor.

Orne felt his body bathed in perspiration. His head ached. His arm throbbed where Maddie had slashed it. His breath came in gasping sobs, as though he had been running.

A bronze clangor echoed behind him. The green wall returned to its featureless gray. Footsteps slapped the floor. Hands worked at the bowl on Orne's head, lifted it gently. The straps that had confined him fell away.

Bakrish came around to stand in front of Orne.

"You said it was an ordeal," Orne panted.

"And I warned you about hate," Bakrish said. "But you are alive and in possession of your soul."

"How do you know if I still have my soul?"

"One knows by the absence," Bakrish murmured. He glanced at Orne's wounded arm. "We must get that bandaged. It's night now and time for the next step."

"Night?"

Orne peered up at the slitted windows in the dome.

They gave him a view of darkness punctured by stars. He looked around the giant room, realized the shadowless exciter-light of glowglobes had replaced the daylight. He said: "Time goes quickly here."

"For some it does," Bakrish sighed. "Not for others." He motioned for Orne to get up. "Come along."

"Let me rest a moment. I'm worn out."

"We'll give you an energy pill when we bandage your arm. Hurry along now!"

"What's the rush? What am I supposed to do now?"

"It is apparent that you understand the two faces of a miracle," Bakrish said. "I observe that you have a personal mystique, an ethic in the service of life, but there is much more to your ordeal and the time is short."

"What's next?" Orne asked.

"You must walk through the shadow of dogma and ceremony. It is written that motive is the father of ethics and caution is the brother of fear . . ." Bakrish paused. ". . . and fear is the daughter of pain."

Silence is the guardian of wisdom, but loud jesting and levity lead a man into his own ignorance. Where there is ignorance there is no understanding of God.

— Sayings of the ABBODS

"He shows a nice restraint," the Abbod said. "I observe that in him: a nice restraint. He doesn't *play* with his powers."

The Abbod sat on a low stool in front of his fireplace, Macrithy standing behind him with the latest report on Orne. In spite of the hopeful words, there was sadness in the Abbod's voice.

Macrithy heard the tone, said: "I, too, observe that he did not call his woman to his side or otherwise experiment with the Great Machine. Tell me, Reverend Abbod, why is it you do not sound happy about this observation?"

"Orne will reflect upon this himself, given time. He will see that he does not need the machine to do what he wills. What then, dear friend?"

"You have no doubts that he *is* the god you called up?"

"No doubts at all. And when he discovers his enormous powers . . ."

"He will come seeking *you*, Reverend Abbod."

"There will be no stopping him, of course. I don't even want it tried. There exists only one challenge I pray he will face."

"We stopped the Speaking Stone," Macrithy ventured.

"Did we? Or did it turn away in amusement, seeing

184

another purpose in existence?"

Macrithy put his hands to his face. "Reverend Abbod, when will we stop these terrible explorations into regions where we have no right to go?"

"No right?"

"When will we stop?" Macrithy lowered his hands, revealing tearstains on his round cheeks.

"We will never stop short of our total extinction," the Abbod said.

"Why? Why?"

"Because we began this way, dear friend. This has begun, it had a beginning. That is the other meaning of discovery. It means to open up into view that which has always been, that which is without beginning and without end. We delude ourselves, you see? We cut a segment out of *forever* and say, 'See! Here is where it started and *here* is where it ends!' But that is only our limited viewpoint speaking."

Order implies law. By this, we indicate the form which helps our understanding of order, enabling us to predict and otherwise deal with order. To go on to say, however, that law requires intent, this is another issue. It does not at all follow from the existence of law. In fact, awareness of eternity opens quite a contrary view. Intent requires beginning: first, the intent and then the law. The essence of eternity is no beginning, no end. Without beginning, no intent, no eternal motive. Without end, no ultimate goal, no judgment. From these observations, we postulate that sin and guilt, products of intent, are not fixed derivatives of eternity. At the very least, such concepts as sin-guilt-judgment require beginnings, thus occur as segments of eternity. Such concepts are ways of dealing with finite law and, only incidentally, with eternal matters. It is thus we understand how limited and limiting are our projections onto Godhead.

—ABBOD HALMYRACH,
Challenge of Eternity

The night air carried a chill nip, making Orne thankful for the thickness of his toga. Bakrish had led him to a large park area enclosed within the religious warren. Birds cooed from trees in the deeper shadows. The place smelled of new-mown grass. There were no artificial lights in the immediate area, but Bakrish followed a rough path as though he could see it and Orne followed the dim outline of the priest's robe.

Ahead of them, a hill stood outlined against stars.

Up the hill marched a snaketrack of moving lights.

Orne's injured arm still ached, but an energy tablet had walled off his weariness.

Bakrish spoke over his shoulder: "The lights are carried by students and each is accompanied by a priest. Each student has a two-meter pole with a lighted box atop it. The box has four translucent sides, each of a different color, as you can see—red, blue, yellow and green."

Orne watched the lights flickering like phosphorescent insects on the dark hill. "What's the reason for all this?"

"They demonstrate piety."

"Why the four colors?"

"Ahhh, red for the blood you dedicate, blue for truth, yellow for the richness of religious erperience, and green for the growth of life."

"How does marching up a mountain show piety?"

"Because they *do* it!"

Bakrish picked up the pace, deserted the path to cross a stretch of lawn. Orne stumbled, hurried to catch up. He wondered again why he allowed himself to follow this *ordeal*. Because it might lead him to the Abbod? Because Stetson had ordered him to carry out this assignment? Because of his oath to the I-A? None of these reasons seemed adequate. He felt trapped on a narrow track which he might leave as easily as Bakrish had left the pathway behind them.

The priest stopped at a narrow open gate through a stone wall and Orne grew aware that a line of silent people was passing through the gateway. Hands reached out from the line to take long poles from a rack beside the gateway. Lights bloomed into existence beyond the wall. He smelled human perspiration, heard the shuffling of feet, the swish of robes. An occasional cough sounded, but there was no conversation.

Bakrish took a pole from the rack, twisted the base. Light glowered from a box at the top of the pole. The box was turned red side toward the procession through the gate. It cast a ruddy glow on the people—student and priest, student and priest, eyes downcast, expressions sober and intense.

"Here." Bakrish thrust the pole into Orne's hands.

It felt oily smooth to Orne. He wanted to ask what he was supposed to do with it besides carry it . . . if anything, but the silence of the procession daunted him. He felt silly holding the thing. What were they *really* doing here? And why were they waiting now?

Bakrish took his arm, whispered: "Here's the end of the procession. Fall in behind; I will follow you. Carry your light high."

Someone in the line said: "Shhhhh!"

One picked out a dim figure at the end of the procession, stepped into line. Immediately, warning prescience sapped his energy. He stumbled, faltered.

Bakrish whispered: "Keep up! Keep up!"

Orne recovered his stride, but still felt the klaxon emptiness in his vitals. His light cast a dull-green reflection off the priest ahead.

A murmurous rhythm began to sound from the procession far ahead, growing louder as it passed down the line, riding over the shuffling and slither of robes, drowning out the chitter of insects in tall grass beside their path. It was a wordless sound: "Ahhh-ah-huh! Ahhh-ah-huh!"

The way grew steeper, twisting back upon itself, a meander line up the hill—bobbing lights, dim shapes, chant, root stumbles in the path, pebbles, slippery places, cold air.

Bakrish whispered at Orne's ear: "You're not chanting!"

The sense of danger, his own feelings of being out of place, combined to fill Orne with rebellion. He whispered back: "I'm not in good voice tonight!"

Ahhh-ah-huh! What utter nonsense. He felt like throwing the light down the hill and striding off into the night.

Line and chanting stopped so abruptly Orne almost collided with the priest ahead of him. Orne stumbled, regained his balance, straightened his pole to keep from hitting someone. People were bunching up all around him, moving off the trail. He followed, breaking a way through a low thicket. There was a shallow amphitheater beyond the thicket, a stone stupa within it about twice the height of a man. Priests began separating from the students, who formed a semicircle flowing down to the stupa. Their lights bounced multicolored reflections off the stones.

Where was Bakrish? Orne looked around, realized he had been separated from Bakrish. What was he supposed to do here? How could this show piety?

A bearded priest came from behind the stupa, stood in front of it. He wore a black robe, a three-cornered red hat. His eyes glistened in the light. The students grew silent.

Orne, standing in the outer ring, wondered how this could be part of an ordeal. What were they going to do?

The red-hatted priest spread his arms wide, lowered them. He spoke in a resonant bass voice: "You stand before the shrine of Purity and the Law. These are the two inseparables in all true belief. Purity and Law! Here is the key to the Great Mystery which leads on to paradise."

Orne felt the tension of his warning prescience and, now, the impact of an enormously swelling psi force. This psi was different, somehow, from what he had experienced before. It beat like a metronome with the cadence of the bearded priest's words, blossoming and amplifying as the passion of his speech increased.

Orne focused on the words: ". . . the immortal goodness and purity of all great prophets! The breath of eternity given for our salvation! Conceived in purity, born in purity, their thoughts ever bathed in purity! Untouched by base nature in all of their aspects, they show us the way!"

With a shock of realization, Orne recognized that this psi force around him now arose not from some machine, but from a mingling of emotions arising out of the massed listeners. He sensed the emotional content, subtle harmonics on the overriding psi field. The bearded priest played his audience like a musician playing his instrument.

"Have faith in the eternal truth of this divine dogma!" the priest shouted.

Incense wafted across Orne's nostrils. A hidden voder began emitting low organ notes, a melody full of rumbling and sonorous passages which came up behind the priest's voice, but never drowned it.

Orne saw a graveman circling the massed audience to the right, priests there waving censers. Blue smoke wafted over the listeners in ghostly curls. A bell tinkled in abrupt cadence as the priest paused. It rang seven times.

Like a man hypnotized, Orne absorbed the whole scene, thinking: *Massed emotions act like a psi force! What is this power?*

The priest at the stupa raised both arms, fists clenched, shouted: "Eternal paradise to all true believers! Eternal damnation to all unbelievers!" His voice lowered: "You, who seek the eternal truth, fall to your knees and beg for enlightenment. Pray for the veil to be lifted from your eyes. Pray for the purity which brings holy understanding. Pray for salvation. Pray for the All-One to cast his benediction upon you."

A shuffling whisper of robes came from the students as they sank to their knees around Orne. But Orne remained standing, his whole being caught up in discovery: *Massed emotions produce a psi force!* He felt elevated, cleansed, standing on the brink of a great revelation. He wanted to call out to Bakrish, to shout his discovery.

Angry muttering flowed through the kneeling students, catching Orne's attention only in part. Glares of protest were directed at him. The muttering grew louder.

Prescient awareness roared within Orne. He came out of his reverie to recognize the danger all around him.

At the far corner of the kneeling crowd a student lifted an arm, pointed at Orne. "What about him? He's a student! Why isn't he kneeling with the rest of us?"

Orne cast searching glances all around. Where was Bakrish? Someone tugged at Orne's robe, urging him to kneel, but Orne backed off. The trail was right behind him through the thicket.

Someone in the massed students screamed: "Unbeliever!" Orne felt the force of it like a psi net hurled across him, dimming his awareness, blocking reason.

Others began taking up the word in a mindless chant: "Unbeliever! Unbeliever! Unbeliever! . . ."

Orne inched his way backward through the thicket, fear sharp within him. The tension of the crowd was a tangible thing, a fuse that smoked and sizzled its way toward a massive explosion.

The bearded priest glared up at Orne, the dark face contorted in the kaleidoscopic gleams of the students' torches. The amphitheater suddenly was a nightmare scene to Orne, a demoniac place, and he realized he still carried his own torch like a waving beacon. Its light revealed the trail beside him leading off into blackness.

Abruptly, the priest at the stupa raised his voice to an insane scream: "Bring me the head of that blasphemer!"

Orne hurled his light like a spear as the students jumped to their feet with a roar. He whirled, fled along the trail hearing the thunder and shouts of pursuit.

As his eyes adjusted to starlight, Orne discerned the trail, a black line on black. He discarded caution, ran all out. A ragged yell lifted into the night from his pursuers. The trail curved to the left and a blotch of deeper blackness loomed at the turn. *Woods?* Branches whipped his face.

The trail dipped, twisted to the right, then left. He tripped on a root, almost fell. His robe caught on a bush and he lost seconds releasing it. The mob was a roaring, waving pack of lights almost upon him. Orne plunged off the trail downhill to his right and parallel to a line of trees. Bushes snagged his robe. He fumbled with the belt, left the robe behind.

Someone above him shouted: "I hear him! Down there!"

The pursuers came to a plunging stop, held silence for a heartbeat. Orne's crashing flight dominated all other sounds.

"There he goes! Down that way!"

They were after him. He heard them breaking through the brush and trees, the curses and shouts.

"Here's his robe! I've got his robe!"

"Get his head!" someone screamed. "Tear his head off him!"

Orne ducked a limb, scrambled and slid down a hill, plunged across the trail and tore his way through a thicket. He felt cold and exposed in only sandals and the light shorts he had worn beneath the robe. Branches clawed at his skin. He heard the mob, a human avalanche on the hill above him—curses, tearing sounds, thumps. Lights waved. Robed figures leaped through the night.

Again, Orne found a trail. It went downhill to his right. He turned onto it, gasping, stumbling. His legs ached. A tight band held his chest. His side ached. The trail plunged him into deeper darkness and he lost the trail. He glanced up to see trees against the stars.

The mob raised a confused clamor behind him.

Orne stopped, leaned against a tree to listen.

"Part of you go that way!" someone shouted. "The rest of you follow me!"

Orne drew in wracking breaths, gasping. Hunted

like an animal because he'd momentarily abandoned caution! He recalled Bakrish's words: *"Caution is the brother of fear . . ."*

Almost directly above Orne and no more than fifty meters away, someone shouted: "Do you hear him?"

Off to the left, an answering voice yelled; "No!"

Orne pushed himself away from the tree, crept down the hill, working his way cautiously, feeling each step. He heard someone running above him, footsteps thumping away to the right. The sound faded. Confused shouts, then silence and then more shouts came from the middle distance on the hill off to the left. These, too, faded.

Sometimes crawling, always testing each step, Orne melted his way through the darkness beneath the trees. Once, he lay flat to allow five running figures to pass below him. When they were gone, he slipped down the hill and across another loop in the trail. The wound on his arm throbbed and he saw that he had lost the bandage. The pain reminded him of the itching sensation he had experienced while strapped in Bakrish's chair. *It had been like the itching experienced when a wound healed—but* before *the wound.*

Orne felt that he had encountered another clue to Amel, but its meaning eluded him.

He fell into a fluid rhythm of flight—under the bushes, avoid leaves, dart through the darkest places where trees blotted out the stars. But the trees thinned out, bushes came farther apart. He felt lawn underfoot, realized he had come down to the last slopes leading into the park area. Dim lights glowed from windows to his right. There was a wall. Orne crouched, hugged himself to still his shivering.

Bakrish had said the Abbod Halmyrach was near-by.

As he thought of Abbod, Orne felt the vacant gnaw-ing within him ease momentarily, then throb stronger. What did that mean? he wondered. Safe . . . but not safe? He experienced a driving desire to find the Ab-bod, to wring the truth from the recognized leader of all Amel.

Why bother with the lower echelons? Where was Bakrish when I needed him? Is this the way a field agent of the I-A operates?

Orne felt he had been freed from a dream. *Dogma and ceremony! What empty nonsense!*

A wolfish grin came over Orne's face. He thought: *I declare myself a graduate of this ordeal! It's over. I've passed the tests!*

Footsteps on a path sounded to his left.

Orne slid behind a tree, peered around it. Through the thin starlight filtered by scattered trees he saw a priest in white moving along a path which would take him directly in front of the concealing tree. Orne flat-tened himself against the trunk, waited. Birds whirred and rustled in the branches overhead. The fragrance of night-blooming flowers crossed his nostrils. The footsteps came closer, passed.

Orne slipped from behind the tree. Four running steps on the soft grass beside the trail, one hand out and around the priest's neck—pressure on a nerve. The priest gasped once, relaxed, slumped in Orne's arms.

Envy, desire and ambition limit a man to the Universe of Maya. And what is that Universe? It is only the projection of his envy, his desire and his ambition.

—NOAH ARKWRIGHT,
The Wisdom of Amel

"What folly!" the Abbod said. "You deliberately told your friend to set the mob on him. And after I expressly forbade it. Ahhh, Macrithy . . ."

Macrithy stood bent-shouldered in the Abbod's study. The Abbod sat in the *lotus* posture on a low table facing the priest. Two fingers upraised in antennae position, knobby knees protruding where he bent across them, the Abbod stared fixedly at Macrithy.

"I was only thinking of you," Macrithy protested.

"You did not think at all!" The Abbod was terrible in his quietly pained judgment. "You did not think of the human beings who were turned into a mob. Orne could have cast them into eternal hell. He might still do it when he comes into his full powers."

"I came to warn you as soon as I knew he had escaped," Macrithy said.

"Of what use is this warning?" the Abbod asked. "Ahhh, my dear friend, how could you have fallen into such error? You see, what is happening right now is the easily predictable consequence of your actions. I

196

can only surmise that *this* situation is what you really wanted."

"Oh, no!" Macrithy was horrified.

"When mouth and action disagree, believe action," the Abbod said. "Why do you want to destroy us, Macrithy?"

"I don't! I don't!" Macrithy backed away from the Abbod, made fending motions with both hands. He stopped when his back encountered the wall.

"But you do," the Abbod said, his voice sorrowful. "Perhaps it's because I assigned Bakrish to Orne and not you. I know it was an assignment you wanted. But it could not be, my friend. You would have sought to destroy Orne . . . and yourself. I could not permit that.".

Macrithy buried his face in his hands. "He'll destroy us all," he sobbed.

"Pray he doesn't," the Abbod said, his voice soft. "Send him your love and your concern for him. Thus, he may come to a fortunate awakening."

"What good is love now?" Macrithy demanded. "He's coming for you!"

"Of course," the Abbod murmured. "Because I summoned him. Take your violence away now, Macrithy. Pray for yourself. Pray for a cleansing of your spirit. I, too, will pray for that."

Macrithy shook his round head from side to side. "It's too late for prayer."

"That *you* should say such a thing," the Abbod mourned.

"Forgive me, forgive me," Macrithy pleaded.

"Take my blessing and go," the Abbod said. "Ask the forgiveness of the God Orne, as well. You may have caused Him great hurt."

Worldly use of power can destroy an angel. This is the lesson of peace. Loving peace and pursuing peace are not enough. One must also love one's fellows. Thus one learns the dynamic and loving conflict which we call Life.

—NOAH ARKWRIGHT,
The Wisdom of Amel

Orne strode down a narrow street in the heart of the religious warren. He hugged the wall and avoided lights, but not with furtive motions. The priest's robe hung loosely on him and a little long. He tucked a fold under his belt, hoped someone would find the priest—but not too soon. The man lay bound and gagged with strips torn from his own underclothing beneath bushes in the park.

Now, to find the Abbod, Orne thought.

Keeping his stride even and calm, he crossed an alley. A sour smell of old cooking tainted the narrow passage. The slap-slap of Orne's sandaled feet made a double echo off stone walls.

Light poured from another alley directly ahead of him. Orne heard voices. He stopped as shadows were projected out of the alley and across the intersection. Two priests came into view. They were slender, blond and benign. Both turned toward Orne.

"May your god grant you peace," Orne said.

The pair stopped, faces in shadows now, the light behind them. The one on the left said: "I pray you follow the path of divine guidance." The other said: "If you live in interesting times, I pray the fact causes you no alarm." He coughed, then: "May we serve you?"

"I have been summoned to the Abbod," Orne said. "I seem to have lost my way." He waited, alert for any movement from this pair.

"These alleys are a maze," the priest on the left said. "But you are near." He turned, throwing a long, hooked nose into profile against the light. "Take this next turning to your right. Follow that way until the third turning on your left. That way ends at the court of the Abbod. You cannot miss it."

"I am grateful," Orne murmured.

The priest who had given directions turned back to Orne, said: "We feel your great power, blessed one. Pray, give us your benedition."

"You have my blessing," Orne said, and meant it.

The two straightened abruptly, then bowed low. Still bowing, the one on the right asked: "Will you be the new Abbod, blessed one?"

Orne put down a sense of shock, said: "Is it wise to speculate on such matters?"

The pair straightened, backed away. In unison, they said: "We meant no harm. Forgive us!"

"Of course," Orne said. "Thank you for directing me."

"A service to one's fellows is a service to God," they said. "May you find wisdom." There was a curious echoing quality to their voices, one slightly out of step with the other. Again, they bowed, then scurried around Orne and hurried on their way.

Orne stared after them until they were lost in darkness. *Curious*, he thought. *What was that all about?*

But he knew how to find the Abbod now.

It is not necessarily loving kindness to build a fence around your master. How then can he observe his servants and see that they minister to him without thought of reward? No, my son, a fence is often a work of fear and a container for dust.

—Sayings of the ABBODS

The street of the Abbod proved to be even narrower than the others. Orne strode down it, observing that he could stretch out both arms and touch the opposed walls. They were rough stone illuminated by widely spaced glowglobes of an ancient design, all black plasteel curlicues around the globes. A door glowed dimly gray at the end of the alley. The area smelled of newly turned earth and fungus. The plastrete surface underfoot was dishmarked with the passage of feet.

The Abbod's door proved to be locked.

Orne thought: *A locked door? Can all be sweetness and purity on Amel?*

He stepped back, peered up at the wall. Dark irregularities atop it suggested spikes or a similar barrier.

Orne's thoughts turned cynical: *Such civilized appointments on this peaceful planet.*

There was violence in this place beyond the ravening of mobs. Narrow alleys were easy to defend. Men who knew how to give sharp orders knew how to give military orders. The trappings of psi and a constant harping on peace betrayed a concern with massive violence.

A concern with war.

Orne glanced back up the alley. It remained empty. He sensed the urgency of the fear within him. A dead-end street could live up to its label. He wanted to leave this place as fast as his feet would take him. This thought brought him no relief from the internal signal. One place was as dangerous as another on this planet. There was no way out of it except to plunge through the danger.

He took a deep breath, shed the priestly robe, swung a hemmed corner up onto the wall, pulled. The robe slipped, caught. He tested it, heard a small tearing sound, but the fabric held. Orne tried his weight on it. The robe stretched, but remained firmly caught atop the wall.

Scrabbling sounds marked his passage up the stones. He avoided sharp spikes at the top, crouched there to survey his surroundings. One window on the top floor of the two-story building opposite him glowed with a dim rose light behind loose draperies. Orne glanced down, saw a courtyard, tall pots in rows topped with flowering bushes. He glanced once more at the lighted window, felt the abrupt stab of rejection.

Danger there!

An air of tension filled the courtyard.

The shadows could hold an army of guards, but an inner sense told him the danger lay in some other source.

Behind that window.

Orne freed the robe from the spike, dropped into the courtyard, crouched in shadows while he slipped back into the garment. Fastening the belt, he worked his way around the yard to the left, avoided the pots, hugged the shadows.

Vines dropped from a balcony below the lighted window. He tested one and it came away in his hands. Too fragile. He moved farther along the wall of the house. A draft fanned his left cheek. He paused, peered into darker blackness: an open doorway.

Warning fear tingled along his nerves. He put it down, slipped through the doorway into a stairwell.

Light flared in the stairwell!

Orne froze, then suppressed laughter as he saw the beam switch beside the doorway. He stepped backward: darkness; forward: light.

The stairs climbed in a curve to the left. Orne moved up them, drifting silently, found a door at the top with a single golden initial: *A.*

The Abbod?

The door handle was a simple short bar on a pivot. No palm-code lock or other device. Anyone could open it. Orne felt the dryness of his throat as he put a hand to the short bar, depressed it. A final click sounded. Orne threw the door open, lunged through and slammed it behind him.

"Ahhh, I have been expecting you."

It was a faintly tenor masculine voice with an edge of quavering to it.

Orne slued around, saw a wide hooded bed. Remote in the bed like a dark-skinned doll sat a man in a white nightshirt. He lay propped against a mound of pillows, the face faintly familiar. It was narrow and with a nose like a precipice over a wide mouth. The polished dark baldness of the head gleamed in the faint light of a single glowglobe beside the bed.

The wide mouth moved and the faintly quavering

tenor voice said: "I am the Abbod Halmyrach. I welcome you and bless you."

An odor of age and dust dominated the room. Orne heard an ancient timepiece ticking somewhere in the shadows.

He took two steps toward the figure in the bed. His prescient sense increased its warning pressure. He paused, placing the familiarity of the Abbod's face. "You look like a man I know as Emolirdo."

"My younger brother," the Abbod said. "Does he still insist on explaining that his name stands for Agony?"

Orne nodded.

"That's a small attempt at humor, you know," the Abbod said. "His name is really Aggadah, which refers to the maxims and such in the Talmud. That's a very ancient religious book."

"You said you were expecting me," Orne said.

"I normally expect the ones I summon," the Abbod said. His eyes seemed to peer through Orne, searching, probing. One skeletal arm lifted, gestured toward a simple chair beside the bed. "Please be seated. Forgive me for receiving you in this fashion, but I find myself jealous of my rest in these latter years. You found my brother in good health when last you saw him?"

"Yes, he seemed healthy."

Orne crossed to the chair, wondering about the Abbod. Something about this frail-appearing and skinny ancient spoke of powers beyond anything Orne had ever before encountered. Deadly forces lay dormant in this room. He glanced around, saw dark hangings on the walls, weird shapes worked upon them—curves

204

and squares, pyramids, swastikas, a repetitive symbol like an anchor fluke.

The floor felt cold and hard. Orne looked down, saw black and white tiles in large pentagonal pieces. Each was at least a meter across. Polished wood furniture stood in the shadowy corners. He identified a desk, a low table, chairs, a visorecord rack with lyre sides.

"Have you summoned your guards?" Orne asked, turning his attention back to the Abbod.

"What need have I of guards?" the Abbod asked. "When a thing is guarded, *that* creates the need for guards."

Again, the skeletal arm gestured toward the chair. "Please be seated. It disturbs me to see you so uncomfortable."

Orne studied the chair. It was a spindly thing without arms to conceal secret bindings.

"It is just a chair," the Abbod said.

Orne sat down like a man plunging into cold water, tensed his muscles to leap. Nothing happened.

The Abbod smiled. "You see?"

Orne wet his lips with his tongue. The air in the room bothered him. It felt deficient to his lungs. Something extremely out of place here. It was not going as he had imagined, but as he reflected upon this, he couldn't think how he had imagined this meeting. It just wasn't right.

"You have had a very trying time," the Abbod said. "It was necessary for the most part, but please share my fellow feeling. I well recall how it was for me."

"Oh? Did you come here to find out some things, too?"

"In a sense," the Abbod said. "In a very real sense."

"Why're you trying to destroy the I-A?" Orne blurted. "That's what I want to find out."

"A challenge does not necessarily imply the wish to destroy," the Abbod said. "Have you deciphered the intent behind your ordeal? Do you know why you cooperated with us in this perilous testing?" The large eyes, brown and glossy, peered innocently at Orne.

"What else could I do?"

"Many things, as you've just demonstrated."

"All right . . . I was curious."

"About what specifically?"

Orne felt something quicken within him, lowered his eyes. As he reacted, Orne wondered at himself. *What am I hiding?*

The Abbod said: "Are you being honest with yourself?"

Orne swallowed. He felt like a small boy called to account by his schoolmaster. He said: "I try to be. I . . . believe I continued because I suspected you might be teaching me things about myself that . . . I didn't already know."

"Superb," the Abbod breathed. "But you're a product of the Marakian civilizations which . . ."

"And the Nathian," Orne interrupted.

"To be sure," the Abbod said. "And this civilization boasts of many techniques for the human to know himself—reconditioning, sophisticated microsurgical resources, the enforced application of acultural toning. How could there be anything about yourself that you still needed to know?"

"I just . . . knew there was."

"Why? How?"

"There's always something more we need to know about anything. That's the way it is in an infinite universe."

"A rare insight," the Abbod said. "Have you ever been afraid without knowing precisely why?"

"Who hasn't?"

"Indeed," the Abbod agreed. "You speak the words, but I do not believe you act upon your insight. Ahhhh, if we only had the time to enroll you in the study of thaumaturgical psychiatry and the ancient Christians."

"Enroll me in what?"

"There were mental sciences long before the techniques developed by your civilization," the Abbod said. "The Christeros religion preserves many fragments of such techniques. You would find such study valuable."

Orne shook his head. This wasn't going the way it should. He felt defensive, outmaneuvered. Yet, all he faced was one skinny human in a ridiculous nightshirt. *No* . . . Orne corrected himself. He faced much more than that. The sense of power here could not be ignored.

The Abbod said: "Do you really believe you came here to protect your precious I-A, to discover if we were fomenting war?"

"That has to be part of the reason," Orne said.

"And what if you discovered that we *were* planning a war? What then? Are you the surgeon? Are you prepared to cut out the infection and leave society in its former health?"

Orne felt a flare of anger which receded as quickly as it had come. *Health?* The concept bothered him. What was health?

"All around us," the Abbod said, "shadowy forces exist. Now and again they break through the encrusting dimensions, and they coalesce into forms tangible enough that we are aware of them. You are aware of such forces right now. If we view them from the viewpoint of life, some of these forces are healthy, some unhealthy. There are ways in which life can speak to these forces, but our communications do not always produce the results we anticipate."

Silently, Orne stared at the Abbod, aware with a ringing sense of hollowness that they had embarked on a perilous course. He felt forces surging within him, wild and terrible.

The Abbod said: "Do you not see parallels between the things we have thus far discussed?"

"I . . ." Orne gulped. "Maybe."

"The best of a supremely mechanistic scientific society weighed you, Orne, and assigned you a niche in its scheme of things. Does that niche fit you?"

"You know it doesn't."

"Something remained in you," the Abbod said, "which your civilization could not touch; just as there always remains something which your I-A does not touch."

Orne felt a lump in his throat, thought of Gienah, of Hamal and Sheleb. He said: "Sometimes we touch too much."

"Of course," the Abbod agreed. "But most of every iceberg remains beneath its sea. Thus it is with Amel.

Thus it is with you, with the I-A, with every manifestation we can recognize."

Again, Orne felt the surge of anger. "These are just words," he muttered. "Nothing but words!"

The Abbod closed his eyes, sighed. He spoke softly: "The Guru Pasawan, who led the Ramakrishnanas into the Great Unification which we now know as the Ecumenical Truce, taught the divinity of the soul, the unity of all existence, the oneness of the Godhead, the harmony of all religions, the inexorable flow of eternity. . . ."

"I've had enough religious pap!" Orne snapped. "You forget: I've been through some of your machines. I know how you manipulate the . . ."

"Consider this in the nature of a history lesson," the Abbod murmured, opening his glistening eyes to stare at Orne.

Orne fell silent, abashed at his emotional outburst. Why had he done that? What pressures were concealed here?

"The discovery and interpretation of psi tends to confirm the Guru Pasawan," the Abbod said. "Thus far, our postulates remain secure."

"Oh?" And Orne wondered at this; surely, the Abbod wasn't going to venture a scientific proof of religion!

The Abbod said: "All of mankind acting together represents a great psi force, an energy system. The temporary words are unimportant because the observable fact remains. Sometimes, we call this force *religion*. Sometimes, we invest it with an independent focus of action which we call God."

"Psi focus!" Orne blurted. "Emolirdo implied I

209

might be . . . well, he said . . ."

"A god?" the Abbod asked.

Orne saw the old man's hands trembling like leaves on the bedcovers. The prescient fear was gone, but he didn't think he enjoyed the surge of internal forces that remained.

"That's what he said," Orne agreed.

"We have learned," the Abbod said, "that a god without discipline faces the same fate in our dimensions as the merest human confronted with the same circumstances. It is unfortunate that humankind has always been so attracted to absolutes—even in our gods."

Orne recalled his experience with Bakrish on the hillside, the mob, the psi forces surging from that massed organism of humanity.

The Abbod said: "You speak with a certain glibness of eternity, of absolutes. Let us turn to finite existence instead. Let us consider a finite system in which a given *being*—even a god—might exhaust all avenues of knowledge, and know everything, as it were."

Orne saw the image painted by the Abbod's words, blurted: "It'd be worse than death!"

"An unutterable and deadly boredom would face such a being," the Abbod agreed. "The future would be an endless repetition, the replaying of all its old records. It would be, as you say, a boredom worse than extinction."

"But boredom's a kind of stasis," Orne said. "That'd break down somewhere and explode into chaos."

"And where do we poor finite creatures make our existence?" the Abbod asked.

"Surrounded by chaos," Orne said.

"Immersed in it," the Abbod said, his old eyelids fluttering. "We live in an infinite system where anything can happen, a place of constant change. Our one absolute: Things change."

"If anything can happen," Orne said, "your hypothetical being could be extinguished. Even a god?"

"Quite a price to pay to escape boredom, eh?" the Abbod asked.

"It can't be that simple," Orne protested.

"And probably isn't," the Abbod agreed. "*Another* consciousness exists within us which denies extinction. It has been called such things as collective unconscious, the *paramatman, Urgrund,* Sanatana Dharma, supermind, *ober palliat.* It has been called many things."

"Words again." Orne objected. "The fact that a name exists for something doesn't mean that thing exists."

"Good," the Abbod said. "You do not mistake clear reasoning for correct reasoning. You are an empiricist. Have you ever heard the legend of Doubting Thomas?"

"No."

"Ahhh," the Abbod said, "then a mortal may instruct a god. Thomas is one of my favorite characters. He refused to take crucial facts on faith."

"He sounds like a wise man."

"I have always so considered him," the Abbod said. "He questioned, but he failed to question far enough. Thomas never asked who the gods worship."

Orne felt his inner being turn over—one slow evolution. He sensed forces falling into place, concepts, order, chaos, new relationships. It was an explosion of awareness, a blinding light that illuminated infinity for him.

When it passed, he said: "You did not instruct Mahmud."

'We did not," the Abbod said, his voice low and sad. "Mahmud escaped us. We may generate gods . . . prophets, but we are not always in a healthy relationship with them. When they point out the pathways to degeneracy and failure, we may not listen. When they indicate the way out of our blindness, veils fall upon our sight. The results are ever the same."

Orne spoke, hearing his own voice echo with a terrible resonance in the Abbod's room: "And even when you follow the *way*, you achieve only temporary order. You climb toward power and fall into shattering circumstances."

An inner light glowed from the Abbod's glossy eyes. He said: "I pray to you, Orne. Have you any count on the number of helpless innocents tortured and maimed in the name of religion during our bloody history?"

"The number is meaningless," Orne said.

"Why do religions run wild?" the Abbod asked.

"Do you know what happened to me out there tonight?" Orne demanded.

"I knew within minutes of your escape," the Abbod said. "I pray you not to be angry. Remember, I am the one who summoned you."

Orne stared at the Abbod, seeing not the flesh but the forces which came to focus there as though pouring through a torn place in a black curtain.

"You wanted me to experience and learn the explosive energy within religion," he said. "Truly, a mortal *may* instruct a god." He hesitated. "Or a prophet.

You please me, Abbod Halmyrach."

Tears poured from the Abbod's eyes. He said: "Which are you, Orne: god or prophet?"

Orne silenced sensory perception, examined the new relationships, then: "Either, or both . . . or none of these. One has a choice. I accept your challenge. I will not start a wild new religion."

"Then what will you do?" the Abbod whispered.

Orne turned, waved a hand. A dancing sword of flame came into being about two meters from his outstretchd hand. He aimed its point at the Abbod's head, saw fear glisten in the old eyes.

"What happened to the first lonely human who tapped this form of energy?" Orne demanded.

"He was burned alive for sorcery," the Abbod husked. "He did not know how to use the force after calling it into existence."

"Then it is dangerous to call a force into existence without knowing how to use it," Orne said. "Do you know what this particular force was called?"

"A salamander," the Abbod whispered.

"Men thought it was a demon with a life of its own," Orne said. "But *you* know more about it than that, don't you, Reverend Abbod?"

"It's raw energy," the Abbod whispered. He drew in a ragged breath, sank back against his pillows.

Orne observed the lapse, infused the Abbod with additional energy.

"Thank you," the Abbod said. "Sometimes I forget my years, but they do not forget me."

"You forced me to accept the things I already could do," Orne said. "I doubted the existence of a superior consciousness which sometimes manifests itself in men, in gods, prophets and machines. But you gave me the test of faith and forced me to have faith in myself."

"It is thus gods are made," the Abbod ventured.

Orne recalled the old nightmare—*"Gods are made, not born."* He said: "You should have listened to Thomas. Gods do worship. I summoned Mahmud and Mahmud was not of your making. I caused pain and suffering. In an infinite universe, a god may hate."

The old man put his hands over his face, moaned: "Ohhh, what have we done? What have we done?"

Orne said: "Psi must be faced with psi."

By willing it, Orne projected himself into space and alternate dimensions, found a place where psi forces did not distract. Somewhere, there was a great howling of nonsound, but he could ignore it. The thought of blazing seconds ticked within him.

TIME!

He juggled symbols like blocks of energy, manipulated energy like discrete signals. *Time and tension: Tension equals energy source. Energy plus opposition equals growth of energy. To strengthen a thing, oppose it. Growth of energy plus opposition produces (time/time,) produces new identities.*

Orne whispered soundlessly to TIME. *"You become like the worst in what you oppose."*

TIME displayed it for him: The great degenerated into the small, priest slipped into evil . . .

Somewhere beyond him, Orne sensed chaotic energy flowing. It was a great blankness filled with ceaseless flowing. He felt himself on a mountaintop and there was a mountaintop beneath him. He pressed the living earth with flattened palms.

214

Thus I have shape, he thought.

A voice came to him from below the mountain. He was being pulled down the mountain, distorted, twisted. Orne resisted the distortion, allowed himself to flow toward the voice.

"Blessed is Orne; blessed is Orne . . ."

It was a persistent chant in the Abbod's voice. There were others then—Diana, Stetson . . . a multitude.

"Blessed is Orne . . ."

Orne *saw* with senses he created for the purpose, and into dimensions of his own making. Still, he sensed the flowing chaos, knowing that even this might not hold him. One had only to make the proper perception. Veils would fall away.

"Blessed is Orne," the Abbod prayed.

Orne felt a pang of sympathy for the old man, recognized the awe. It was like Emolirdo's aborted demonstration—a three-dimensional shadow cast into a two-dimensional universe. The Abbod existed in a thin layer of time. Life projected the Abbod's matter along that thin dimension.

The Abbod prayed to his God Orne and Orne answered, coming down from the mountaintop, erasing the worship of the multitudes, coming to rest as a physical form cross-legged and seated upon the bed.

"Once again you summon me," Orne said.

"You have not said which you choose," the Abbod said. "God, prophet . . . or what?"

"It's interesting," Orne said. "You exist within these dimensions, yet outside them. I have seen your thoughts blaze through a lifetime, taking only a second for the journey. When you are threatened, your awareness retreats into no-time; you force time almost to a standstill."

The Abbod still sat propped up in bed, but now he held his hands extended prayerfully. He said: "I pray that you answer my question."

"You already know the answer," Orne said.

"I?" the Abbod's eyes opened wide in surprise. The thin old shanks trembled in the bed.

"You have known it for thousands of years," Orne said. "I have seen this. Before men first ventured into space, some were looking at the universe in the right way and learning to answer such questions. They called it *Maya*. The tongue was called Sanskrit."

"Maya," the Abbod whispered. "I project my consciousness upon the universe."

"Life creates its own motive," Orne said. "We project our own reason for being. And always ahead of us—the great cataclysm and the great awakening. Always ahead of us—the great burning time from which the phoenix arises. The faith we have is the faith we create."

"How does that answer my question?" the Abbod pleaded.

"I choose that which any god would choose," Orne said.

And he disappeared from the Abbod's bedroom.

As Orne indicated, the prophet who calls forth the dead actually returns the body's matter to a time when it was alive. The man who walks from planet to planet sees time as a specific location; without time to stretch across it, there is no space. Orne has created our universe as an expanding balloon of irregular dimensions. Thus he accepted my challenge and answered my prayer. We can continue staring at our universe through the symbol-grids which we construct. We can continue reading our universe like an old man with his nose pressed against the page.

—Private report of the
ABBOD HALMYRACH

In his Marak office, Tyler Gemine, director of R&R, faced his visitor across an immense blackwood desk. The desk smelled of a perfumed polish. Its wide top held a holographic projection of Gemine's family and a communications console.

Behind Gemine, a simulwindow looked out across the pyramid steps of Marak's Government Central, a descending line of parks and angular structures glistening under the green light of noon sun. The director was a rounded outline against the simulwindow, a fat and genial surface with smiling mouth and hard eyes. Frown wrinkles creased his forehead.

"Let me get this clear, Admiral Stetson," Gemine said. "You're telling me that Orne *appeared* in your office out of nowhere?"

Stetson slouched in the shaping chair across from

Gemine, eyes almost level with the desk top. It interested him that the polished surface of the desk created an illusion of heat waves which danced across Gemine's chest.

"That's what I'm telling you, sir," Stetson said.

"Like that fellow from Wessen, you mean? A psi thing?"

"Call it whatever you want, sir: Orne just popped out of nowhere, grinned at me and delivered that message."

"I don't find this flattering at all," Gemine protested. His hard eyes bored into Stetson.

Stetson hid amusement under a mask of concern. "Well, sir, there are a lot of us from I-A who need jobs now that you've taken over our work."

"I understand that," Gemine said, his gaze cold and measuring. "But I resent, I *deeply* resent the suggestion that R&R has been making dangerous mistakes . . ."

"There was that unfortunate business on Hamal, sir," Stetson said, "not to mention Gienah and . . ."

"I am *not* suggesting we're perfect, Admiral," Gemine said. "But our positions now remain pretty clear. The vote in the Assembly was decisive. The I-A is no more and we are . . ."

"Nothing's really decisive in a final sense, sir," Stetson said. "You'd better, ahhh, kind of go through once more what Orne is saying in that message."

"His message is plain enough," Gemine said. "And I must say it sounds rather farfetched to suggest that I should take this on faith and . . . I say, isn't it getting rather hot in here?" Gemine ran a finger around his collar.

Without shifting his body, Stetson pointed to the region above Gemine's left ear.

The R&R director turned, eyes going wide as his gaze encountered a dancing point of flame hanging in the air. Burning, prickling sensations crawled along his skin. Abruptly, the flame swelled to a ball almost a meter in diameter.

Gemine leaped to his feet, knocked over his chair as he stumbled backward. Heat blasted his face.

"How now?" Stetson asked.

Gemine dodged to the right and the flame shot ahead of him, cutting him off. It pressed him toward a corner.

"All right!" Gemine shrieked. "I agree! I agree!"

The flame dwindled to a spark, vanished.

"The way Orne explains it," Stetson said, "there's no place in the universe where there hasn't been flame at some time or other. It's just a matter of shifting space and time so the space coincides with a time of fire. As long as we've come to an agreement, you can sit down, sir. I don't think he'll bother you anymore unless . . ."

Gemine righted his chair, sank into it. Perspiration ran from his face. He stared at Stetson with a stricken expression, said: "But you said I was to remain in charge of the department!"

It was Stetson's turn to scowl. "Damn nonsense about hoes and handles!"

"What?"

"He says we live in a universe where anything can happen and that means even *war* has to be a possibility," Stetson growled. "You've read the report! We didn't dare leave a thing out of his message."

Gemine glanced fearfully at the area over his left ear, back to Stetson. "Quite." He cleared his throat, leaned back and steepled his hands in front of him.

Stetson said: "I'm to be attached to your office as a special executive assistant. My duties are to facilitate the absorption of I-A into . . ." He hesitated, swallowed. ". . . R&R."

"Yes . . . of course." Gemine leaned forward, his manner suddenly confidential. "Any idea where Orne is now?"

"He said he was going on a honeymoon," Stetson growled.

"But . . ." Gemine shrugged. "I mean, with his powers, with the things he apparently can do . . . I mean, the psi thing and all . . ."

"All I know is what he told me," Stetson said. "He said he was going on a honeymoon. He said it was the thing any normal, red-blooded man would want to do at a time like this."

Once a psi, always a psi. Once a god, you can be anything you choose. I give you the proper obeisance, Reverend Abbod, for your kindness and your instruction. Humans get so conditioned to looking at the universe in terms of little labeled pieces they tend to act as though the universe really were those pieces. The matrix through which we perceive the universe has to be a direct function of that universe. If we distort the matrix, we don't change the universe; we just change our way of seeing it. As I told Stet, it's like a drug habit. If you enforce anything, including peace, you require more and more of that thing to satisfy you. With peace, it's a terrible paradox: You require the contrast of more and more violence, as well. Peace comes to those who've developed the sense to perceive it. In gratitude for this, I will keep my promise to you: humankind has an open-ended account in the Bank of Time. Anything can still happen.

—LEWIS ORNE to the Abbod Halmyrach

P.S. *Please record a note that I want this inscription on my tomb: "He chose infinity one finite step at a time." We'll call our first son Hal and let him make up his own joke about what it means. I'm sure Ag will help him.*

Love, L.O.